TORIA

Margaret MacWilliams

A CANDLELIGHT EDWARDIAN SPECIAL

To Ella Mae MacWilliams

Published by
Dell Publishing Co., Inc.
1 Dag Hammarskjold Plaza
New York, New York 10017

Dell ® TM 681510, Dell Publishing Co., Inc.

ISBN 0–440–19031–2

Printed in the United States of America

First printing—August 1981

A

CANDLELIGHT EDWARDIAN SPECIAL

CANDLELIGHT REGENCIES

TORIA

Prologue

She was born on May 24, 1870, in an undistinguished stone house on one of those narrow, wretched alleys under the shadow of London Bridge, close to the murky Thames where the constant clamor and movement of the river never ceases.

At the moment of her birth, far across the city on the Horse Guards parade ground, the Prince of Wales was reviewing the spectacular trooping of the colors, honoring his mother's birthday. Queen Victoria, a stout, doughty little woman in somber black, remained at Buckingham Palace, mourning the death of her beloved Albert, preferring that her son participate in the endless round of ceremonies which were as much a part of the life of the royal family as the solemn tolling of Big Ben on the quarter hour.

As the midwife had predicted, it proved to be a difficult birth. When it was over, the young girl lying on the low, lumpy cot was too weak to hold the child in her arms.

"It's a girl, Letty," her sister Ann said, crouching beside the bed and clasping the tiny infant in her arms. "And I believe she is blessed with your golden hair."

Letty Leighton managed a rueful, twisted smile.

"How unfortunate," she whispered, "if she resembles me."

"What do you intend to name her?" Ann asked the question urgently, frightened by the deadly pallor on her sister's face as her eyelids fluttered for a moment and closed.

"Victoria." Letty's reply was so low, Ann could scarcely catch the word. "For isn't today the queen's birthday?"

Ann Leighton felt hot tears course down her cheeks. "Victoria Leighton," she murmured. "What a lovely name, but far too fancy for the likes of us. We'll call her—Toria."

Sighing, the midwife bent over to cover the face of the young girl with a blanket and, as she waited impatiently for her money, muttered, "It never pays for the likes of us to become too fancy. If your sister Letty here had learned that lesson, she'd still be alive. Did she never tell you who the father was?" Her hard, beady eyes glinted with curiosity.

Stiffening, Ann cradled the infant, who had begun to whimper, more closely to her breast. "Never," she replied.

"A toff, I reckon." The midwife placed a tattered shawl over her head, preparing to ease her huge bulk out of the narrow room. "You'd better teach this little one early on her place in life," she advised. "If not, she'll end up like her mother." Shaking her head mournfully, she stepped out onto the crowded, dirty street, making her way laboriously to her next delivery.

Chapter One

There is something about the advent of spring that affects the gamut of society—from the poor to the rich, from the old to the very young. Even in the heart of the city, it changes the tempo of life as the grass in the park turns green, as the tender buds on the trees unfold, and the air becomes warm and fragrant, inviting one to throw off the winter doldrums with a tantalizing promise—that around the next corner there might be a fresh new world to discover.

It was May 24, 1886, and as Toria Leighton returned from an afternoon of marketing at Billingsgate and Petticoat Lane, she found it impossible to walk at a decorous pace, preferring to skip now and then along the narrow cobbled streets. She was balancing her purchases in one hand, with the other deep in the pocket of her skirt, clutching the coins Aunt Ann had given her that morning as a birthday present.

I should buy material for a new dress, she told herself sternly. That is what Ann expects me to do. But the prospect of cutting, stitching, and sewing a frock to wear only to church on Sundays did not appeal to her in the least, for after all, today she had turned sixteen, a most important landmark, and she

9

felt that surely there must be a more exciting way to spend the money.

She paused at the corner leading to their alley, entranced by a poster plastered on the side of the streetlamp, advertising the pleasures of an evening spent at the Alhambra. Soaked by the spring rains, it had become tattered and stained, but she could still make out the chorus line of women dressed in bright-colored costumes, laughing as they kicked their legs high in the air.

"You like that, don't you, Miss Toria?"

She turned swiftly, recognizing the voice of Mr. Tobey, the cobbler, whom she considered an old friend. When she passed his shop each morning on her way to school, he never missed giving her a smile and a wave, while often in the afternoons when she went to market, she lingered for a time to admire his workmanship and exchange pleasantries.

"Oh, yes," she breathed. "Have you ever been there, Mr. Tobey?"

"Every so often I take the Missus. We enjoy the music and the comedians. One needs a laugh now and then, don't you agree? It makes the next day go faster."

"We're going tonight," he added. "Want to come along?"

Toria hesitated, torn between duty and desire. "I have the money," she said finally, "and it's my birthday, but—"

"But what?" he broke in. "You need a bit of fun in your life, Miss Toria. So think it over and be here by seven, if you decide to come. It's a long trip across the river to Leicester Square."

Toria nodded, moving onward, making her way

up the crooked alley, absorbed in her thoughts, completely unaware of the picture she presented to passersby. She had yet to realize that she was a breathtakingly beautiful girl on the threshold of womanhood—her luxuriant golden hair tumbling to her shoulders and her eyes a deep violet, haunting, intelligent, and mysterious. Her every movement was graceful and proud.

"She walks as if she thinks she's a duchess!" Her grandfather often remarked with asperity.

But there was more to her appearance than sheer loveliness and an aura of the aristocrat, for she possessed an inner glow that lifted the spirits of everyone she encountered. She was like a brilliant peacock among the sparrows, and there were a multitude of sparrows on the crowded streets of London.

Reaching the stone house halfway up the hill, where she had been born and lived all of her life, she entered. It seemed to her that the stiff parlor and tiny kitchen were shabbier and more dismal than ever. She could not bear to spend another evening there, an evening which would be exactly the same as all the others—her grandfather seated across from her at supper, dour and disapproving, while her aunt tried valiantly to make small talk, recounting the frivolous chatter of the wealthy clients at Lucille's, where she worked as a seamstress.

With an air of defiance, Toria dumped her packages on the table in the kitchen as she made up her mind to go with the Tobeys to the Alhambra and worry about the consequences later.

When Toria, escorted by Mr. and Mrs. Tobey, reached the Alhambra, they were jostled by a throng of eager theatergoers, vying to gain admission. Enthralled by the elaborate gilded facade with its profusion of minarets and turrets glistening in the lamplight, she became completely unaware of the people pushing and shoving around her, certain she was about to enter a world of enchantment—eager yet somewhat fearful to take her first step into the unknown.

"Come along, dearie," Mrs. Tobey cried out, giving Toria a good-natured shove which jolted her back to reality. "It's everyone for himself unless you want to be trampled upon."

The promenade confused and frightened her at first—the bars with their tiers of bright-colored bottles, the painted ladies openly accosting the men, the noise, the loud laughter—but her fear was short-lived when the Tobeys guided her behind the railing to join the stolid family groups who had come to listen to the music and to watch the dancers and comedians.

Soon she was so involved with what was happening on stage as one act followed the other, she forgot that she had been frightened and began to entertain the errant thought that this was where she belonged, this was what she was meant to do.

All too soon, it was over, and they left the bright lights of the theater for the dark, teeming streets with the night noises surrounding them—the shout of cabbies jockeying for position, the aged, feeble crones peddling flowers, and the prostitutes with their brazen glances promising an hour or two of lovemaking for a shilling or a bottle of wine.

"This is no place for a young girl!" Mrs. Tobey stated firmly, finding it necessary to shout in order to be heard above the hubbub.

"Nonsense," her husband replied, "Watching the performers leave is the best part of the whole evening."

Standing in the shadows near the stage door, they saw the glamorous women of the theater in their glittering gowns, claimed by men in shiny top hats and evening clothes before being whisked away in open carriages.

"How beautiful!" Toria exclaimed, so caught up in the magic of the moment, she had forgotten the existence of the Tobeys, and as she moved away from them under a streetlamp hoping for a better view, the hood of her cape fell back, exposing her golden hair, her ripe lips slightly parted, her violet eyes, electric with awe and excitement.

"Beautiful is right!" A man's voice declared. "Mark my words, Alex, soon this one will outshine them all."

Two men in evening attire stood before her, the shorter one who had spoken giving her a formal, slightly mocking bow, while the other, tall, erect and very elegant, threw his companion an impatient glance as he said with a frown, "Beautiful, yes, but far too young to be alone at night on the streets of London."

"But I'm not alone, sir," she answered airily. "I'm with the Tobeys."

"In that case," he answered with a smile, "We must find the Tobeys immediately."

The streetlamp outlined his handsome, aristocratic features, but it was his eyes, more than anything else, that drew her to him—they were dark brown, remarkably large and eloquent, and losing herself momentarily in their depths, she felt not only

13

warmth and compassion in them but a hint of wonder and admiration.

She smiled at him in return, a tremulous, unsteady smile, and then with a toss of her head replied pertly, "Oh, I can take care of myself."

As the Duke of Blakesley watched the Tobeys and the young girl vanish into the darkness, he addressed his companion with considerable anger. "I swear, Dickie, if I had not been here, you would have attempted to seduce the girl."

"Undoubtedly, I would have made the attempt," the Earl of Hadley replied with extreme insouciance, "and in retrospect, my dear Alex, I am beginning to heartily regret that I inveigled you into accompanying me to the Alhambra this evening, for I might have known that you with your high principles, recently betrothed to one of England's great heiresses, would never have stooped to such frivolity."

"Certainly not, particularly at the expense of someone so recently out of the cradle," the duke retaliated severely. "That lovely child was so touching and innocent that only a complete boor could contemplate taking advantage of her."

Dickie Hadley lit a cigar, drew on it deeply, and with a laugh signaled for his carriage. "So be it, Alex," he replied. "You win, as you usually manage to do. Therefore, let us repair to my club for a nightcap, and while we linger over glasses of brandy, perhaps you'll explain to me why you consider the state of matrimony the proper, the only course to follow."

Chapter Two

The dishes had been washed and put away, the oil lamps cleaned and replenished, yet Ann Leighton found it impossible to ease herself into a chair and rest her aching feet. She was alone in the house. Her father had long since departed for his nightly libation at the local pub, leaving her to wonder where Toria could possibly be.

She had returned home from work at seven o'clock to find a fire laid in the hearth and a cold supper set out on the kitchen table. She had expected at any moment to hear the front door slam and Toria's lilting greeting echoing through the empty rooms.

But instead, the girl had not returned, and now, as Ann Leighton peered out the small-paned windows into a swirling fog, she could not shake the dreadful premonition that something disastrous had occurred. Toria had been frequently instructed never to be out after darkness had fallen, and up until tonight she had always complied with the warning.

It was after ten o'clock when she heard her father's heavy footsteps on the pathway leading to the house. When he entered and asked if Toria had returned, she lied to him for the first time in her life, saying lightly, avoiding his eyes, "My yes, long since. She was delayed at the market. She's gone to bed."

Ann heaved a sigh of relief when he hung his coat on a rack in the kitchen, stretched, yawned deeply, and with a curt "Good night" climbed the creaking staircase to the second floor.

It was bordering on eleven o'clock when Toria at last appeared, opening the front door quietly, her slim figure concealed by a dark woolen cape, its hood covering her glistening curls.

"Where have you been?" Ann demanded sharply, her anger mixed with sheer relief that Toria had returned apparently unharmed. During the past few hours, she had conjured up vivid pictures of the girl floating on the Thames or stretched out on a slab in some chilly morgue, the victim of an unidentified assailant.

"Oh, Ann, I'm dreadfully sorry." Toria removed her cape and, tossing it on a chair, spun lightly about the room. "It was wrong of me, I know, terribly wrong, but I did something I have wanted to do for a very long time. I went to a music hall."

"Alone?" her startled aunt inquired.

"No, with Mr. Tobey and his wife. Ann, it's a fairyland—the music, the dancing, the gaiety were so entrancing, I could hardly bear it. Don't worry. We shunned the promenade and at all times were surrounded by a very decent crowd. Afterwards, we watched the performers leave the theater—the women so glamorous in their marvelous gowns being met by men in shiny top hats and evening clothes. We stayed there in the shadows to the very end. I couldn't tear myself away, and the Tobeys were very kind to wait with me until the last carriage departed.

16

I never knew before that such an exciting world existed."

"Where did you find the money for a ticket?" Ann Leighton demanded, wanting but unable to believe that Toria was telling her the full truth.

"You'll be angry, I know. I spent the birthday money you gave me to buy material for a dress, but I really don't care about that, Ann, for my old clothes will be quite all right, as I seldom go anywhere."

Crossing to the stove to heat water for tea, Ann sighed. It was true the poor child seldom went anywhere, and she was such a gay, lighthearted creature, not meant to lead a drab, uneventful life.

Sensitive and intelligent, Ann knew Toria had realized early on that for some mysterious reason her grandfather disliked her. He seldom smiled at her, never caressed her, and only acknowledged her presence when reproving her for some minor infraction.

Over the years it had taken a great measure of skill on Ann's part when the girl asked the inevitable questions, to gloss over the truth, telling her that her mother had died in childbirth, that her father had died soon thereafter, and that the family, especially her grandfather, had never recovered from the shock.

"And he blames me for my mother's death," Toria had often remarked sadly.

While Ann would invariably reply, "No, darling, he doesn't blame you for it—he's simply unable to accept the fact that she is gone. You remind him constantly of her. It's unfortunate he reacts the way he does, but it's not your fault."

The kettle whistled, and turning from the stove, Ann said, "We must talk. Are you hungry?"

"No, I'm far too excited to even think of food."

Ann sighed again. "Well, at least have some tea. You are most fortunate that I told your grandfather you were already in bed, and he believed me. I can imagine all too well how enraged he would be if he had the slightest suspicion of where you went tonight."

Toria's face clouded over, as it always did at the mention of her grandfather. With a shiver, she said, "Sometimes the way he looks at me is quite frightening."

Ann poured hot water into the pot and left the tea to steep, busying herself collecting cups and spoons, reluctantly reaching the conclusion that the time had come to tell this child she loved so much the sordid details of her mother's tragic death.

Toria sipped her tea, her huge violet eyes never leaving her aunt's face as she joined her at the wooden table. "I think," she finally remarked solemnly, "that I am now old enough to be told the true story."

It was quiet in the kitchen for several moments before Ann answered, and when she did, the tears slid unchecked down her careworn face. "Your mother," she began, "was much like you, perhaps not quite so lovely. When you walk into the room or sing in church on Sundays, I often catch my breath, believing you to be Letty. You are that alike."

"What really happened, Ann? You must tell me." Toria brushed aside the fact that she resembled her mother and had inherited her unusually fine singing voice. It was something she had been told many times in the past, a compliment used, she suspected, to avoid telling her the truth.

"Letty," Ann finally said, "against your grandfather's wishes, became involved in the theater. She was a Gaiety Girl. When he found this out, he banished her from the house. You must be aware of the reputation those women have. He wouldn't tolerate it. I believed we would never see Letty again, until she returned to have her baby. I guess she had nowhere else to go—so she came back hoping for forgiveness."

"Which she did not receive?"

Ann shook her head sorrowfully. "No, except from me. Our love for each other never changed."

"And my father?" Toria persisted. "Where was he during all this? Why didn't he help my mother out? Did he die soon after she did, as I've been told?"

Ann shifted uneasily in her chair, replying in a low voice, reluctant to look at her niece directly. "I told you he died because I wanted to protect you—I didn't want you to be hurt. Perhaps it was wrong of me to do so. I don't know whether he is alive or dead, for she never told us his name."

"So I'm a bastard. I've suspected it for some time."

Ann felt a shudder run through her body. "Don't say that word," she said harshly.

"Why not? For it's true and I believe one should always face the truth. I wonder who he was? Do you suppose I'll ever discover his name?"

"It was sixteen years ago. I very much doubt it. So now you understand why your grandfather is severe with you. Every time he sees you, it reminds him of what he considers a great disgrace."

19

The clock in the kitchen chimed eleven thirty. Ann, rising wearily, began to collect the dishes. "Go to bed very quietly," she warned, "for if your grandfather learns where you have been, I can't answer for the consequences."

Toria nodded her head and, as if in a dream, started toward the staircase. But before she ascended, she turned back to her aunt and said with a tender smile, "Thank you, Ann, for being honest with me."

After Toria had gone Ann stood at the sink, deep in thought, neglecting to begin washing the dishes, realizing how foolish she had been to delay making a decision regarding Toria's future. She had known for some time that the girl must go to work, but up until now she had shied away from taking the first step, in her heart reluctant to condemn the child to long hours in some squalid factory or bent over a table at Lucille's shop.

But now, because of what had happened tonight, Ann knew an immediate decision was absolutely necessary, and that Toria must be kept so busy that there would be no time to dream about the music halls, to yearn for the brilliant lights of the theater, where reckless women threw away their virtue for a glamorous existence that all too often ended in disaster. It had been Letty's undoing, and Ann was determined that Toria must be prevented at all costs from following in her mother's footsteps.

Perhaps the position of a maid in some nobleman's household would be preferable, she decided. Although the pay was notoriously low, very little time was allotted to the servants in the great houses to cast even a passing glance at the outside world. She recalled too that only that afternoon the Marchioness of Esterbrook, while at Lucille's for a fitting, had been loudly and bitterly complaining to all who would listen that excellent servants were becoming more and more difficult to obtain. "Why young girls prefer the factory, I can't imagine," she had exclaimed as Ann knelt beside her, pinning the hem of one of Lucille's latest creations.

Yes, Ann concluded, that might be the best solution, for she knew without question that it was imperative that Toria Leighton leave her grandfather's house without delay.

In the small upstairs bedroom, Toria undressed quickly, blew out the candle, and climbed into bed. Although she was exhausted after her long evening at the Alhambra followed by the shock of Ann's revelations, sleep nonetheless eluded her as she turned and twisted restlessly in her narrow cot.

The music she had heard during the performance still haunted her, and closing her eyes, she visualized herself in the center of the stage, not a part of the chorus, but alone, singing to an audience that had grown strangely silent, captivated by her talent and beauty.

Hadn't the man who had approached her afterwards outside the theater called her beautiful? She gave a little shiver, recalling the boldness in his glance as in the glow from the streetlamp his eyes had raked her face. What would have happened, she wondered, if the Tobeys had not been nearby or if the other gentleman had not intervened on her behalf?

But it was the other gentleman, whose companion had called him "Alex," who dominated her thoughts. How extremely handsome he was—a trifle stern perhaps, somewhat aloof, but nevertheless during their brief encounter, she had sensed that he had, for one delightful moment, been drawn to her as she had been drawn to him.

Alex. What a splendid name, and how unfortunate that in such a big, bustling city as London the chance of their meeting again was virtually impossible.

Without question, she concluded that he was a member of the aristocracy—his voice, his appearance, every gesture had clearly indicated that. Had her father, she wondered, been a member of the aristocracy too? She suspected he had, for to her it was inconceivable that her mother would ever have given herself to a stodgy middle-class man like her grandfather or her uncles. And if this were true, at least on her father's side she had inherited the bloodline of a titled personage. Maybe that was the reason for her instinctive rejection of her lowly station in life.

When the door finally opened with a creak as Ann came to bed, Toria was still wide awake, every nerve in her body taut and vibrant.

"Ann," she whispered, "is it so wrong for me to yearn for gaiety and excitement?"

Ann sighed deeply as she eased her tired body into bed. "Not wrong," she replied slowly. "Once, long ago I had the same yearnings. The trouble is that what the likes of us desire is out of reach. We're born into a certain class, and we are destined to live and die there."

"What will happen to me? I detest the thought of working at Lucille's, to end—" Toria broke off, ashamed to realize that she had been about to say, "to end my days like you"!

Ann smiled in the darkness and, reaching across

to the girl's bed, patted her shoulder sympathetically. "Don't be afraid to say what you think," she said soberly. "I can't blame you for being reluctant to follow my example. No, for you it won't be Lucille's —I couldn't stand it. Don't worry, I'll find something else for you that will be less confining. We'll talk about it soon—when I return from work tomorrow evening."

Too tired to think any more, Ann fell asleep, and as Toria at last slept too, in her dreams she was in the arms of a handsome stranger named Alex, who held her closely and tenderly as they waltzed together in a huge ballroom that seemed to stretch to infinity.

Chapter Three

The Marquess of Esterbrook's London residence was situated on Park Lane—a stunning Regency structure five stories high, of glistening white marble, with bow windows. A graceful wrought-iron fence shielded its impressive entrance from the street.

It was a clear May day, and the Marchioness of Esterbrook was seated in the morning room overlooking a walled-in garden, its brick path bordered by yellow daffodils still glistening from last night's rain.

Despite the beauty of the day and the sparkle of the sunlight spilling through the mullioned windows, Estelle Esterbrook found herself unable to shake a mood of depression which had gripped her ever since their recent return to London. Up until now she had been completely content with the even flow of her existence, enjoying to the fullest each London season, when her social calendar was crammed with a variety of activities—from fittings at Lucille's and Worth's to teas and receptions at the great houses sprinkled throughout Mayfair, not to forget the balls, the theater, and the races.

For many years now she had been amazed at how swiftly the days and nights passed by, with August

24

arriving almost on the heels of May, when it was time to move to their country estate for the grouse shooting.

Although the marchioness was well aware of the reason for her despondency, so far she had been unable to find an answer to her problem, for what in the world, she wondered despairingly, does one do with a daughter who has turned out to be as unattractive as an old shoe, when no amount of expensive gowns, elaborate coiffures, and lessons in the arts of dancing and music were able to bring about a miraculous transformation.

Faced with such a problem and no solution, it seemed to Estelle Esterbrook grossly unfair that her son, Piers, Viscount Covington, had inherited her dark good looks, while Clara, the poor child, unfortunately resembled her husband, Charles. Not that Charles wasn't a dear, of course he was, with a great amount of charm, but despite all that, one could not overlook the fact that his irregular, hawklike features and sparse, mouse-colored hair, bequeathed by him to Clara, did nothing to enhance his only daughter's appearance.

Yes, she thought with a sigh, Piers was, if anything, far too handsome, far too dashing, and enjoying a trifle too much his regimental assignment with the Blues of the Royal Horse Guards. It was relatively easy for a viscount, even if he were homely, to make his mark in society, and Piers with his amazing good looks, vivacity, and unlimited bank account had, to say the least, from the very outset been a smashing success. Not that she begrudged him this success. On the contrary, she was very pleased about it. Nevertheless, there was no use denying it made it considerably more difficult to launch a daughter who not even by the wildest stretch of the imagination could be classified as attractive.

Clara's debut during the Little Season had been carefully orchestrated by her parents. She had been presented at court along with the other debutantes, and the Esterbrooks had staged an elaborate ball to introduce her to society. Because of their position, she had been included in all of the young crowd's activities that began in October and lasted well into December, but her dance programs had never been completely filled, and without the aid of Piers, who must have browbeaten many of his fellow officers, the family would have been hard put to round up a sufficient supply of escorts.

Also there had been no offers of marriage, not even a single hint of a proposal, with the result that for the first time in her life Lady Estelle had felt a surge of relief when they retired to Essex to celebrate the Christmas holidays. But unfortunately it had been only a temporary relief, for now another season had commenced, and the miserable problem of Clara's future was haunting her all over again.

Frowning, Estelle Esterbrook tossed the footman an irritable look when he entered the morning room and announced a Miss Leighton had arrived for her appointment.

"Miss Leighton," the marchioness muttered and then said, "Oh, yes, do show her in," recalling that one of the seamstresses at Lucille's had only yesterday persuaded her to interview a niece of hers who was seeking employment.

Despite some uneasiness over the prospect of becoming a servant, Toria's natural high spirits bobbed to the surface as she rode in a hansom cab toward London's West End, a section of the city which, up until today, had remained as out of reach to her as the stars in the sky.

First off, it was a marvelous spring morning; secondly, it was her maiden voyage in a carriage; and in addition to all that, who could possibly be gloomy while clip-clopping along wide, tree-lined streets, past stately buildings and luxuriant parks that up until today she had never suspected existed?

The cabbie was in a carefree mood too, turned out in a smart double-breasted yellow greatcoat and shiny top hat, with a scarlet bow on his whip. Therefore, as they drove along Piccadilly toward Hyde Park, she allowed her imagination to run rampant, pretending she was a wealthy young heiress, the daughter of, at the very least, a duke, and that her dress, instead of a rough cambric, was a smooth, iridescent satin, while the bonnet covering her golden curls was a soft velvet with a cluster of white feathers blowing gently in the breeze. And, of course, there must be a handsome gentleman seated beside her, so people passing by on the street would pause to stare and watch with envy as their carriage rolled along.

She became so carried away by her fantasies that she was brought back abruptly to reality when the hansom cab came to a sudden halt, and the driver announced in a sonorous tone that they had arrived at the residence of the Marquess of Esterbrook.

Dressed discreetly in a simple black frock patched and rusty with age, her old woolen cape concealing her cascade of glistening curls, Toria passed through

27

the wrought-iron gates and took three deep breaths before gathering enough courage to lift the brass knocker on the white door.

The servant who opened it, splendid in his green and gold livery, flashed her a disdainful look before asking her why she didn't know enough to go to the servants' entrance, finally shrugging his shoulders with resignation as he instructed her to follow him.

The marble floor in the hallway was as smooth as a skating rink, and as she walked behind the footman, she gathered a jumbled impression of soft rugs that one's feet sank deeply into, of tables and chairs of every conceivable size and description, and massive oil paintings on every wall, framed in ornate gold.

By the time she eventually reached a room which she later learned was called the morning room, she had become so thoroughly confused and frightened that it took her several seconds to still the wild beating of her heart and realize that she was in the presence of what Ann always called a great lady. For the Marchioness of Esterbrook was without a doubt a most imposing figure. Her hair, still black and glossy, was piled high on her head in the latest fashion, her large, dark eyes were cold and penetrating, and in a white lace peignoir that was voluminous and seemed to float about her like a cloud, the only word that could describe her adequately was *imperious*.

"Well," the marchioness was saying in a cool, clipped voice, observing Toria closely through her tortoiseshell lorgnette, "according to your aunt you are an expert seamstress. Now tell me, is that the truth?"

"Yes, milady." Toria almost whispered her reply,

overpowered by so much splendor to the point where she was considering flight.

"What other talents do you possess?"

"I know how to cook and clean house, and I love to sing," the young girl burst out.

Estelle Esterbrook's dark eyes widened in surprise. "I doubt very much," she said drily, "if you will be called upon to entertain us, but we do need additional help. As you can see, this is a very large, active establishment. Therefore, if you wish to join our staff, we'll give it a try. Your wages will be six pounds a year with every other Sunday off. Our housekeeper, Mrs. Stackhouse, will be the one to spell out your duties. Uniforms and bed and board will naturally be provided."

"It sounds very fair, milady," Toria ventured.

"It is very fair," the marchioness replied, emphasizing the word *is*. "We'll expect you to report for duty at seven o'clock tomorrow morning, and next time use the proper entrance." With a curt nod of her head, she indicated the interview was over.

No sooner had Toria departed, trailing behind the stern, erect figure of the footman, than the marchioness once more turned her thoughts to the future of her daughter, Clara, forgetting immediately the young, frightened girl who had stood before her only a few moments ago. To Estelle Esterbrook it had been a completely unimportant incident, while for Victoria Leighton it proved to be the beginning of a new and challenging life.

Chapter Four

From the outset Toria Leighton found the housekeeper, Mrs. Stackhouse, formidable. A tall, angular woman with iron-gray hair pulled back severely into a bun at the base of her neck, she rarely permitted herself or any member of her staff to smile.

With her pale, flinty blue eyes, she inspected her newest employee carefully from head to toe, swiftly concluding she was far too pretty and far too fragile to survive. Allotting her one week, two at the most, before dismissal, she fervently wished the Marchioness of Esterbrook would allow her free rein in deciding who and who not to employ.

Toria, as she listened intently to the housekeeper's rapid instructions, was quick to sense that she had somehow failed to measure up to her rigid standards and that she had already acquired a potential adversary. With a defiant lift of her determined chin, Toria met Mrs. Stackhouse's withering glance squarely, vowing then and there to prove the woman's judgment to be wrong.

Her first impression of the Park Lane residence was of stairs—there were so many of them. On the lower floors they were wide and impressive, constructed of white marble, but as you climbed higher, they became narrower and steeper, while the flight to the top floor, where the servants were quartered, was built of cheap wood, chipped, scarred, and dimly lighted.

Her room on the fifth floor was shabby, minuscule, and unattractive, containing an iron cot with a limp mattress, an ancient bureau, a cracked mirror suspended over it, one straight chair, and a flimsy wardrobe for her clothes. A small window streaked with dirt overlooked the rear of the house onto the mews.

As she changed quickly into the uniform that had been provided for her—a gray cotton dress with a voluminous white apron and a starched white cap that completely covered her golden curls—she felt as if she had just been condemned to a long prison term at Newgate. It took every ounce of her considerable supply of courage not to bolt immediately.

In addition, she soon had dispelled the romantic notion that she would at least be in the wings watching the glamorous life-style of the very rich. In fact, during the first two weeks, she caught only an occasional glimpse of the Marquess and Marchioness of Esterbrook, while their daughter, Clara, she heard only once from behind the closed doors of the music room, singing in a thin, quavery voice. As for the son, Lord Covington, if he had put in an appearance at all, she had failed to witness it.

She discovered also, to her dismay, that the servants functioned in a highly formal manner. Snobbery seemed to be their middle name, the first footman, for example, looking down with disparagement on his inferiors, while Mrs. Stackhouse, at the very top of the scale, treated all and sundry with utter disdain.

31

The only positive aspects of her miserable existence were that the quality of the food was excellent and after a few days of frigid treatment by the staff, one of the upstairs maids made the first feeble overtures of friendship. Her name was Sophie, and she not only began to transmit to Toria all the succulent pieces of gossip from both upstairs and downstairs but rescued her from the brink of many pitfalls resulting from her naïveté and ignorance.

On her first free Sunday, Toria walked in Hyde Park with Sophie—a plump, cheerful country girl who confided to her as they shared a bench by the Serpentine that she had a mad passion for one of the stableboys.

It was a warm, sunny day in June, and as they sat there, Toria began to relax for the first time in many days. The waters of the Serpentine sparkled in the sunlight. Small boats were sprinkled upon its surface, while couples strolled leisurely along the shaded pathways or stretched themselves out on the velvety grass. It was altogether a delightful spot, and Toria, who had never been in the country, imagined it must be somewhat like this.

"Do you expect to marry this stableboy?" she asked her friend with curiosity.

Sophie shook her head gravely. "How can we? It's impossible. First off, old Stackhouse would disapprove and fire me. Also, how could we live on four pounds a year? That's what Ralph earns, currying the horses and polishing the equipage day after day."

"It isn't fair," Toria burst out. "They have so much, and we have so little. I'm beginning to believe I would be better off working in some factory, for once you see how the other half lives, it makes your own poor lot more difficult to bear."

Sophie's eyes widened in surprise, appalled by her friend's violent reaction. "It does no good at all to talk that way," she said with severity. "You'll only make yourself miserable, my girl. Besides, having money and position in society doesn't make one necessarily happy. Look at Lady Clara. She's in misery most of the time, and His Lordship has such bad dyspepsia that he's always taking off for Homburg or Marienbad for the cure. As for Her Grace, she worries constantly over finding a husband for her daughter."

"Would that I were Clara," Toria murmured.

Sophie smiled at her companion, feeling a quick stab of jealousy as she observed how beautiful she was in her blue cotton dress, her golden curls tumbling to her shoulders.

"Ah, you'd be a success, no doubt of that," Sophie said.

"What is the son like, the viscount?" Toria asked.

"As handsome as his sister is homely. He's a bad one though."

"What do you mean by that?" Toria asked.

"Exactly what I said. He loves them and leaves them—chorus girls, actresses, the lot. Why, only last year he got one of the servant girls in trouble. Of course, it was hushed up very quickly. She was with us one day and gone the next. But for two weeks or more, old Stackhouse rampaged around the place, her face like a thundercloud. So watch out for Lord Covington, Toria. Stay out of his sight if you can, for he's alert to spot a lovely figure and face."

Toria laughed. "Don't worry about that. Somehow, someway I intend to make my mark in the world, and no viscount, no matter how dashing, is going to have his way with me. Come on, let's walk a bit beside the water."

Pulling Sophie to her feet, they strolled along the Serpentine, with Toria returning to her world of fantasy where she met Lord Covington, who fell violently in love with her. When she rejected his advances, he became so distraught that in desperation he went to his parents, who reluctantly granted their permission for her to marry him.

"What are you dreaming about?" Sophie asked curiously as she watched Toria's lips curl in a triumphant smile.

But Toria refused to answer, merely shaking her head as she pointed to a family of ducks who were making their way downstream, with the mother out in front proudly leading her flock. "They're lucky," she said. "They don't have to polish and dust someone else's house, and they've never heard of the word *aristocracy!*"

"What a strange girl you are, Toria!" Sophie exclaimed. "Aren't you aware that many members of the upper class are fine, upstanding individuals with high principles and morals?"

"I expect that is true," Toria conceded, "for I met one of them not long ago who rescued me from an absolute bounder. It was outside the Alhambra." Her eyes were sparkling as she recalled the tall, impressive stranger called Alex. "Someday," she continued with a defiant toss of her head, "I plan to marry one of them—a viscount, or a marquess or perhaps even a duke."

Sophie burst out laughing. "Dreams never hurt

anyone, my friend," she responded lightly, "so dream on if you must. But remember—the trouble begins when you try to make such dreams a reality."

Chapter Five

Much to Mrs. Stackhouse's surprise, Toria Leighton survived the first four weeks of her employment, accepting without a murmur the innumerable duties assigned to her and accomplishing her tasks exceedingly well—to the point where the housekeeper could find nothing to criticize.

Nevertheless, Mrs. Stackhouse still kept a close eye on her newest employee, having good reason from past experience to be uneasy if one of the young maids turned out to be pretty. In this case, as Toria was not merely pretty but beautiful, even when wearing a capacious apron over her long gray dress and a dust cap which concealed her glorious hair, Mrs. Stackhouse did not relax her vigilance.

Toria was assigned to mundane tasks—dusting the formal drawing room cluttered with tables crowded with family photographs and bric-a-brac, laying fires in the damp bedrooms, polishing the silver, or, as if that were not enough, carrying the heavy canisters of steaming water to fill the metal bathtubs.

From early morning until dusk, Toria was kept busy, and after supper she was expected to retire to the small sewing room on the top floor of the house to tackle the piles of servants' uniforms that always seemed to be in need of repair.

It was Tuesday, the housekeeper's day off, when Toria was ordered by the head butler to assist him in serving the luncheon. Mrs. Stackhouse would have never permitted such a thing to happen, especially if she had known that Viscount Covington was expected to join his family for the noon meal. But then Mrs. Stackhouse was not present, and while Toria changed into a black uniform, tied a brief frilly apron around her waist, and placed a wispy white cap with streamers on her luxuriant hair, the housekeeper was sipping tea and eating piping hot crumpets at her favorite tearoom, blissfully unaware that the ingredients for a catastrophe were about to be thrown together at the Marquess of Esterbrook's splendid town house on Park Lane.

When Toria reported for duty, Philipps, the butler, irritated that the maid who usually assisted him had become suddenly ill, gave his instructions curtly. "Remove the service plates, keep the water glasses filled, and remove all the dishes when everyone is finished," he said.

Toria nodded her head, temporarily speechless, overawed by the dining room with its magnificent Waterford chandeliers and dramatic dark red damask wall coverings, with a lace cloth on the long table as delicate as a spider's web and the silver bowl in the center filled with pale pink roses and tender green ferns. Therefore, it wasn't until she had removed the service plates that she absorbed the fact that for the first time she was in the same room with Lord Covington and Lady Clara.

The conversation during luncheon was light and

frivolous, mainly centering around a ball that was to take place at Almack's that evening.

"I would be willing to do most anything to avoid attending," Lady Clara protested.

"Nonsense, it's expected of you," her brother responded lightly. "Don't keep underestimating yourself so, Clara. I know of one gentleman who would be despondent if you didn't put in an appearance."

"Who?" The Marchioness of Esterbrook asked eagerly, her large dark eyes fastened on her son with great maternal pride.

"I'm not revealing his name. For the present, he prefers to keep it a well-guarded secret."

Clara, apparently completely uninterested, sighed deeply and remarked that she heartily wished August were here so they could repair to the country and escape the boredom of so many dances.

Her duties accomplished for the time being, Toria stood in a corner of the dining room and had her first chance to study at close range this man who Sophie had told her was such a rake. He was undoubtedly extremely handsome, with short-cropped dark curly hair and a marvelous smile that she could only describe as melting. His eyes were a brilliant blue under heavy brows. He was broad-shouldered, lean, and fit, and the prospect of the possibility of seeing him one day in his cavalry uniform made her almost faint. It was quite obvious that his mother and his sallow-complexioned sister adored him, and if he had any faults, Toria was certain they would be the last to acknowledge them, his mother, particularly, literally fawning on every gesture he made and every word he uttered.

In contrast, Lady Clara appeared dull, lifeless, and

awkward in her movements. Poor girl, Toria thought with compassion—how dreadful it must be to have such a lackluster personality, and not to be able as yet to capture even one beau. It was common knowledge among the servants that as a debutante Lady Clara had been a dismal failure, begging her parents without success to allow her to remain on their country estate to avoid facing further humiliation.

It was late evening, the luncheon at which Toria had served long since over, and she had performed a goodly number of stultifying chores before she was free to go to her room. She considered it her castle, without question a very lowly one, but nevertheless the only place where she could dream her own dreams and think her own thoughts.

Tonight she could think only of Viscount Covington. Piers! What a beautiful name. As she repeated the name aloud, she realized how ridiculous it was to imagine, even for one moment, that he would ever be aware of her existence.

Acknowledging that Sophie had been absolutely right when she warned against attempting to transfer dreams into reality, she still felt there must be some way to escape the monotonous existence of a servant girl. Sophie and the others might be willing to placidly accept a life of servitude, but not she.

Crossing to the cracked mirror above her bureau, she saw the reflection of a great beauty, who even in a shapeless gray cotton dress moved with unusual grace. I won't be a servant girl for very long, she assured the girl in the looking glass. Just you wait and see!

Chapter Six

The music room held a particular fascination for Toria Leighton. The rosewood piano standing in lonely splendor on a raised platform was so highly polished that you could see your reflection, while the ivory keyboard glistened.

For some time now she had been terribly tempted whenever she entered the room to strike a note or two, but it was not until the morning after her first encounter with Viscount Covington that she gathered up enough courage to do so. She had been instructed by Mrs. Stackhouse to dust the music room, and when she discovered that no one else seemed to be nearby, she touched a few keys, softly at first and then more firmly, soon unable to resist echoing the sounds with her clear, bell-like voice.

Startled when she heard someone clapping, she swung about, finding herself face to face with the man whom yesterday at the luncheon table she had found so entrancing.

Blushing a fiery red, she cried out breathlessly, "I'm sorry, milord. I meant no harm."

"Why apologize for having such a lovely voice," he replied, lightly tossing her a gay, debonair smile, and noting with amusement that she was trembling from head to foot. "Tell me, what is your name?"

"Toria."

"Well, Toria, pray honor me with a song." He gave her a low, mocking bow. He was wearing a pearl-gray morning coat with striped trousers and, as he leaned lazily against the side of the piano, she caught her breath, almost overpowered by the brilliance of his blue eyes.

"I can't play the piano," she stammered. "The only songs I know are the hymns I've heard in church."

"What a pity!" He shook his head as if in deep despair. "Such talent ought not to be wasted. You should have lessons."

"Lessons on six pounds a year?" she asked in amazement. "Why, I suspect Lady Clara's music teacher charges close to that for only a few hours of his time."

"Yes, I suspect he does, and what a shame too, for my sister dislikes music with a passion and would much prefer to be riding her horse down some country lane or along Rotten Row. Do you realize, by the way, that in addition to singing like a nightingale you're quite smashing?"

His eyes had never left her face, and now he began to study her figure slowly and with great deliberation, saying with a laugh, "Even with that absurd apron tied around your waist, I can tell you're extremely well put together."

To her dismay Toria blushed again and, disturbed by his boldness, moved away from him. But he followed close behind and, before she could escape,

41

spun her around and pulled her dust cap from her head.

"Your hair is too glorious to hide," he murmured, watching the thick, golden curls cascade about her face until they reached her shoulders.

Thoroughly frightened by now, she swiftly drew away from him and with a quick curtsey fled from the music room, running pell-mell down the corridor that led to the stairs and the safety of the kitchen below.

As she entered the kitchen with a rush, Mrs. Benedict, the cook, a stout, affable woman of an indeterminate age, turned from the stove and threw her a curious glance. "Finished your dusting so soon?" she asked. "Well, if that's the case, sit down and have some tea."

Still trembling, Toria hurriedly put on her white cap, tucking her thick hair under it as best she could.

"Was His Lordship pursuing you?" Mrs. Benedict asked, joining Toria at the kitchen table, and casting a sympathetic smile in her direction as she watched the young girl struggle to regain her composure.

"Yes," Toria replied in a low voice.

"Then stay away from him. He's gotten more than one servant girl in trouble these past few years and lord knows how many actresses and chorus girls. Don't you become the next one!"

"He's so very handsome, yet bold," Tory replied, grateful when the rapid beating of her heart began to slow down and she was able to raise the cup of tea to her lips with a steady hand.

"Handsome—that he is, and a rake of the worst sort too," Mrs. Benedict declared with some heat. "I must warn you that if Mrs. Stackhouse had the slightest suspicion that he was showing an interest in you, she'd see that you packed your belongings and left this house before nightfall."

"Please, you won't tell her," Toria begged. "I need the work."

Mrs. Benedict leaned across the table and gave her a reassuring pat on the shoulder. "Of course I won't tell her. Do you think I'd want to be the cause of having you lose your position? I'm simply warning you that whenever you see His Lordship headed in your direction, you head the other way."

"I will—I promise."

"And lock your door at night," Mrs. Benedict advised.

"Oh, yes, thank you. I'll be most careful," Toria said fervently.

Mrs. Benedict finished her tea, and as she rose from the table to return to the stove, she added one last piece of advice. "If he tells you he is in love with you, don't you believe one word of it."

Toria nodded her head in agreement, making a valiant effort to dismiss from her mind once and for all the delicious sensation of lassitude that had crept over her when the Viscount had stretched out his hand and removed her cap, thankful now that she had been wise enough to flee from his presence when every nerve in her body had been telling her to stay, to discover how it would feel to be embraced by such an attractive, dashing man.

Chapter Seven

It was unusual for Estelle Esterbrook to indulge herself to the point of having breakfast in bed, but this particular morning she did. She had spent a wretched night, with sleep eluding her. Everything this season seemed to be going awry. Last night Clara had returned home early from the ball at Almack's with a set, cold expression on her face, refusing to discuss what had occurred, while Piers had stayed out extremely late. Heaven knows when he had come in. She was certain he was again scheming to have or was already having another sordid little affair that always ended unpleasantly.

It was past time that he married, but on the frequent occasions when she and Charles brought up the subject, he became as skittish as a colt, refusing to discuss the list of prospective brides they had drawn up.

When he tapped on her door this morning and asked to come in, he found her propped against a heap of pale pink satin pillows, listlessly playing with a piece of toast.

"I came to say good-bye," he said, bending over to kiss her cheek. She noticed with a stab of envy that last night's revelry had taken no toll of him—at least on the surface, although she could smell brandy on his breath.

"Back to the regiment," he said cheerfully, sitting on the edge of her bed and taking a sip from her coffee cup.

"Where did you go last night after the ball?" she asked.

He only smiled and shook his head teasingly, saying, "Now, Mother, that's a question you should never ask."

"But we're concerned about you, Piers. Both your father and I believe you should be married. You're past twenty-one, you know. You should be settled down and raising a family."

He scowled and crossed restlessly to the windows, pulling back the curtains and staring down at the street below.

"Clara came home from the ball looking like a thundercloud," the marchioness continued. "I'm at my wits' end to know what to do with her. In addition, her personal maid has given notice, and now I must find someone to replace her."

"Problems—problems," he said lightly and then added in a more serious tone, "Mother, why don't you leave Clara alone? Let her stay in the country if she wants to. Don't you see there's no way you can make her into a popular debutante or post-debutante or whatever her status is at this stage of the game? If she must have a personal maid, and I suppose she must, why not pick someone closer to her age who might give her some companionship along with her duties. Old Wilberforce was ancient enough to be her grandmother and a crashing bore."

"Do you have anyone in mind?" his mother asked.

"As a matter of fact I do—that young girl who waited on table at luncheon yesterday, for example. Why not give her a chance? She looked full of spirit to me. At least she wouldn't hang about Clara with a doleful expression, saying 'my poor child' all the time."

Estelle Esterbrook finished her coffee with a sigh. So yesterday he had noted the girl's beauty, but in all fairness she was not surprised that he had, for she too had been startled by her amazing appearance. Vaguely recollecting the brief interview she had had with her only a few weeks ago, she could not recall thinking at the time that the girl had given promise of such great beauty. Perhaps it was the way she had been dressed that day, so primly and properly in a black dress and shapeless woolen cape.

"Stay away from her, Piers," she warned as her son tossed a contrite look in her direction.

"I will, Mother, I promise. No more peccadilloes, at least on the family premises. Remember, I've already given you my solemn oath to that. I only meant to say it would be good for dear Clara to have someone about her age for her personal maid. But, of course, it's your decision to make.

"Oh, another bit of news," he said, switching the subject suddenly. "Jamie Harrington danced four times with Clara last night, and he confided in me not so long ago that he would not be adverse to becoming an ardent suitor."

"Lord Harrington," Estelle Esterbrook mused. "Not as high a rank as I would wish, and rather poverty-stricken. What was Clara's reaction?"

"She can't abide him, and I must say I don't blame her. He's no intellectual, rather light in the brain

46

department, but he's a good chap overall, well liked in the regiment, rather fun to rack around with."

The marchioness pursed her lips, deep in thought. "Perhaps we should invite him to Sutherland House in August."

"He'd be most pleased. I can vouch for that."

Bending over the bed, he gave her a farewell kiss. "See you on my next free day," he promised, "when we'll talk seriously about my future wife. I agree with you, Mother, it's past time. Believe it or not, I'm growing weary of my bachelor state."

With a carefree wave of his hand, he left her bedroom, closing the door gently behind him. The Marchioness of Esterbrook, considerably mollified, rang for her maid, requesting her to prepare her bath.

Suddenly, despite her miserable night, she felt relaxed and rested. A talk with her son, Piers, even if the topic might be an unpleasant one, never failed to restore her good humor, and today she considered their meeting highly productive. Much to her surprise, he had at last agreed to discuss the subject of his marriage, and he had also promised to honor his pledge not to interfere again in the life of any member of her household.

In addition, the prospect of a suitor in the wings for Clara was highly encouraging, even though Lord Harrington was not the type of husband she would have selected. It was unfortunate, too, that apparently Clara did not look favorably upon him. She shook her head sadly—such a stubborn girl.

As her maid removed the breakfast tray and pulled back the satin coverlet, Estelle Esterbrook decided that perhaps Piers had been right when he had advised her to let up on her relentless drive to make Clara a social success. Perhaps also it would be wise to assign a personal maid to her daughter who was both young and attractive and might be more sympathetic to Clara's multitude of problems.

Chapter Eight

The staff in a large household like the Marquess of Esterbrook's followed as rigid a social structure as Victorian England. Therefore, the reaction to Toria's rapid promotion from one of the most lowly of its members to becoming Lady Clara's personal maid was composed of shock, envy, and downright disapproval. But as it had been the decision of the marchioness, no one was foolish enough to dispute it outright, although there were many mutterings and moanings below stairs.

Only Mrs. Benedict suspected Lord Piers's fine hand in the surprising selection, and although she was careful not to bruit her surmise about, it was quite obvious to her that Toria Leighton as Lady Clara's personal maid would be more in the limelight and more available for His Lordship to scrutinize than as a servant girl relegated to downstairs dusting or dreary chores in the scullery.

At the outset Toria was nervous about her new assignment, fearful that she would not please Lady Clara, that their temperaments might clash, but she soon realized there was no need for her to be afraid. She discovered that her mistress had a very loving, warm disposition. Terribly shy, she appeared at first meeting to be aloof, even austere, but in reality, when one grew to know her, she proved to be exactly the opposite.

Despite the fact that nothing could be done to make Lady Clara into a beauty, as time went on and the two girls learned to admire and trust each other, Toria persuaded her not to dress her hair in complicated curls and ringlets, but to wear it simply brushed back from her face in soft waves and gathered into a large chignon. She also convinced her mistress to select dresses that were simple and classical in line. Gradually there emerged a young lady who never would be considered pretty by the standards of the day, but who was developing a style of her own which was unusual and very chic.

Toria, who spent many evenings in the great houses escorting Lady Clara to and from various functions, loyally concluded that she much preferred Lady Clara's straightforward manner and modest personality to the flock of silly, giggling young debutantes who hadn't a thought in their heads but to capture the attention of some eligible man until he found himself betrothed and on his way to the altar. She realized they had been groomed with that one goal in mind since birth, which made Toria even more inclined to applaud her mistress's independent spirit, which lay beneath a shyness and insecurity that her mother's grim determination to make her a 'success' had merely served to intensify.

During those days in London as she waited on Lady Clara, serving breakfast in her room when she desired it, preparing her bath, and assisting in dressing her for some social activity, they began to laugh and chat together, with Lady Clara opening up a new world for her maid—the world of books—as Toria began, whenever she had an idle moment, to learn how stimulating it was to sample the contents of a novel from one of Lady Clara's overflowing bookshelves.

Shyly at first and then gathering confidence, she began to discuss with her mistress what she was currently reading, discovering that Lady Clara was not only extremely intuitive but intelligent as well.

"A friend of Piers seems to be claiming a goodly number of my dances," Lady Clara remarked to Toria one morning as she ate her breakfast and watched Toria laying out her costume for the morning.

"That must please you," Toria remarked.

"Well it does and it doesn't. It's a relief not to sit with the chaperones and be classified as the wallflower of the season, but I simply don't like him. In fact, I can't stand him. I'm dreadfully afraid he intends to become serious."

"Is he handsome?"

Lady Clara shrugged her shoulders. "Tolerably—not a patch on Piers. But I wouldn't mind if he were ugly, if he were interesting and had some character. Next time when you escort me to Almack's I'll point him out to you. His name is Lord James Harrington. Piers calls him Jamie."

Lady Clara yawned and sighed deeply. "How I wish I could go riding this morning instead of two long hours in the music room."

"Why do you dislike music so?" Toria asked, wondering how in the world anyone could fail to be entranced by the opportunity to learn to play the piano and to sing.

"I don't dislike music," Lady Clara replied. "In fact, I enjoy the opera and musicals very much. It's simply that I am not talented and to me it seems stupid to try to make me so."

"You've improved on the piano a great deal," Toria remarked. "I heard you just the other day when I passed by the music room."

"Yes, I guess I've mastered the keyboard so that when called upon to perform I won't disgrace myself —but I just can't sing. Tell me, do you like music, Toria, or does it bore you?"

Toria blushed. "I love it," she said simply. "I think I've never been happier then when singing hymns in church. Unfortunately, I don't have much chance for that anymore."

After that they turned to another subject, but the next time Lady Clara was scheduled for a music lesson, she suggested Toria join her. For an hour Toria sat quietly in a corner of the music room, completely enthralled.

Monsieur Etienne, the singing instructor, was a thin, nervous little Frenchman, always turned out in a shiny black suit with a frilly white shirt, his bald head glistening with perspiration as he struggled valiantly to teach a pupil who made scant progress, despite her desire to please him.

This morning he so forgot himself as to raise his hands in despair, clutching the few wisps of white hair he still possessed, wailing loudly, "Mademoiselle, that is not right, that is not right at all!" Immediately becoming contrite and apologizing for his outburst, he was relieved when his pupil replied quietly, "I know Monsieur Etienne, you are absolutely justified in your criticism."

Lady Clara, turning to Toria, who thought they had completely forgotten her presence, said impulsively, "Why don't you try the song, Toria? You've told me how you love to sing."

Monsieur Etienne struck the first chord and Toria, crossing to the piano, sang the piece from beginning to end, her beautiful voice, soft and melodious, reaching the high notes with ease, forgetting completely everything but the rapture of the melody and the great delight in being accompanied by an excellent pianist.

As the last note faded and died, Lady Clara clapped her hands with enthusiasm, while Monsieur Etienne sat quite still, his fingers resting on the keyboard, before saying with grave formality, "You have a unique talent, mademoiselle."

Toria blushed, remembering the other time a few weeks ago when Lady Clara's brother had applauded her singing and when she had run from the music room, confused and distraught.

"Thank you," she said. As she returned to her seat in the far corner of the room to listen to the rest of the lesson, she wondered if she would ever encounter Viscount Covington again. She had seen him once or twice since then, but only from a great distance, and she was beginning to question if perhaps Mrs. Benedict's devastating account of his character that day as they drank tea in the kitchen had been something of an exaggeration.

Chapter Nine

On her third Sunday afternoon off, Toria returned to
her grandfather's house for a visit. After the large,
airy rooms on Park Lane to which she had grown
accustomed, the modest stone dwelling near London
Bridge seemed in contrast to her new surroundings
even more cramped and shabby than she had remembered. John Leighton greeted her in his usual cold
and distant manner, leaving the house soon after her
arrival, while she and Ann shared tea and cakes in
the kitchen, with Toria proud to be able to tell her
aunt that she was now Lady Clara's personal maid.

"I probably won't be able to see you again for quite
some time," Toria said regretfully when they parted,
"for plans are already being made to move to the
country."

Leaving her grandfather's house, she strolled
across London Bridge, taking a horse-drawn bus on
the other side. It was a torrid summer's day, so she
sat on top in the open air, welcoming a cool breeze
which occasionally blew in from the river. Fascinated by the colorful sights and sounds of the city, the
jostling crowds on the street below, the vendors peddling their wares, she left the bus at Piccadilly Circus
and, reluctant to end her all too brief holiday, paused

to listen to an organ-grinder whose trained monkey was performing for a group of interested spectators. She was about to move on in the direction of Hyde Park Corner when someone grasped her arm, and startled, she looked up into the face of Viscount Covington.

"As we appear to be going the same way," he said in a leisurely tone, "why don't we walk along together?" He had spent the afternoon at his club, The Guards on Pall Mall, and finding himself both bored and restless, had dismissed his carriage in order to obtain some exercise.

Still grasping her arm, he guided her along Piccadilly. "I want to apologize," he said, breaking an awkward silence, "for frightening you the other day in the music room when you darted away like a scared rabbit. You didn't give me a chance to explain."

"Explain what?" she asked, casting a timid glance in his direction.

"To explain that I had an overwhelming desire to remove your cap merely to admire your lovely hair. Let me assure you that my intentions were strictly honorable. You see, I am not as wild a character as I am sure the servants have pictured me to be. Is it so very wrong to enjoy great beauty?"

"No, there's certainly nothing wrong in that," she agreed.

"I am forgiven then?"

"Yes, you are forgiven." She smiled up at him and found herself dazzled once more by the brilliance of his eyes, amazed to discover he did not appear to be the ogre Mrs. Benedict had described. The pressure of his hand on her arm was warm and comforting, and she was disappointed when she saw the wide green stretches of the park not far ahead of them—a signal to her that this unexpected encounter must soon reach a conclusion, for she knew it would never do to approach the Park Lane town house in his company.

"It's too fine an afternoon to end so soon," he remarked, and she did not resist when he guided her away from Park Lane toward a path leading to the Serpentine. "Let's sit for a while," he said. "And I beg you to remove your bonnet. I promise to be extremely circumspect, to only look and admire, not to touch."

Smiling, she removed her bonnet, thinking at the time how fortunate it was that she was wearing her best frock, a soft blue silk that Ann had fashioned, as it was highly becoming, clinging to her slender body and outlining her soft curves and budding breasts.

"That's much better," he said. "Now tell me about yourself—what part of London you come from and how you happened to gain employment in my parents' household."

It was all so delightful, so innocent, to be sitting beside him on the park bench in the warm sunlight, telling him the brief story of her life.

When she was finished, they continued to sit there in a contented silence, one of a group of many young couples enjoying each other's company. She made no protest when he reached out and gathered her hand in his.

"I like you very much, Toria," he murmured. "You'll never know how refreshing it is to be with a girl who hasn't the least desire to flirt, who is straightforward and sincere in addition to being extremely intelligent."

"You make me sound incredibly dull," she said pertly. "Why do you assume I have no desire to flirt? Believe me, given the opportunity, I would enjoy it immensely."

His eyes were dancing as he slipped his arm casually across her shoulders. "So you do have spunk after all," he remarked. "When you ran away from me the other day, I thought, well, she's like all the rest of them, afraid of a little harmless fun."

"I consider a light flirtation perfectly acceptable," she replied, tossing him a challenging glance, "But I must warn you, milord, I am not the sort of a girl to succumb to a man who regards every woman he meets as fair game. I could never be that foolish."

He laughed ruefully. "I suppose you believe all of the stories you have been told about me?"

She nodded her head emphatically. "Yes, as they seem to be well documented."

"All right," he conceded, "I admit to the reputation of being a bit of a rake, although at the same time I must point out that my exploits have been considerably exaggerated. How would you respond if I were to assure you that my greatest desire in life is to find someone I can truly love and cease my wayward ways?"

Her eyes were dancing now too. "I would say it was a lot of poppycock," she replied, stealing a glance at him, curious to observe his reaction.

"I bow to your superior wisdom," he said with mock formality. "But as we at last appear to understand each other, do you suppose within the near future we can repeat this delightful interlude?"

"I think it highly likely, as we live in the same household."

It was late afternoon. There were fewer boats on the Serpentine, fewer couples strolling along the shaded paths or lying in the lush green grass, but to Toria time had become meaningless as she fervently wished this day, this hour, this moment to go on forever.

It was he who at last suggested they should part. She continued to sit on the park bench long after she had watched him vanish from view, reluctant to break the spell which still surrounded her, knowing she had been playing with fire, but nevertheless glad she had not been prim and proper, ordering him never to approach her again. She examined her hand, which still felt warm from his touch and, rising slowly, left the park immersed in a cloud of euphoria.

Climbing the stairs to her small, threadbare room overlooking the mews, she recalled his remark that he wished to find someone he could truly love, and although she continued to dismiss this declaration as poppycock, she was intrigued by the possibility that maybe she possessed the power to ensnare the dashing viscount in a trap so deep that he would be unable to escape. Was such a scheme so ridiculous, she wondered? It was obvious he was smitten, and if she continued to refuse to surrender to him, wasn't there the outside chance that he would find he could not live without her?

When Sophie burst in to ask if she had enjoyed her day off, it was on the tip of her tongue to confess that she had spent a goodly part of it with Viscount Covington, until a small warning bell cautioned her to keep their meeting a secret. Sophie would only scold and call her indiscreet and spoil the perfection of the time she and Lord Piers had shared.

Chapter Ten

Toria had her first view of the English countryside when she, along with some of the other servants, boarded a train at Paddington Station and started northward to Essex. Sophie, country-bred, was highly amused by her friend's exclamations of delight as they chugged past meadows where sheep and cattle peacefully grazed, stopping at every station along the way—some burgeoning factory towns, bleak and unattractive, their utilitarian buildings besmirched by dust and grime; others small storybook villages, ancient, timeless, replete with histories reaching back to the long-ago days of the Roman occupation.

At Winston, a sleepy community still engaged in rubbing the sand out of its eyes, wagons awaited beside the track to carry them to the Marquess of Esterbrook's estate, which lay some three kilometers east of the town.

As they clattered along cobblestone streets, soon leaving the village behind them for a country road, despite the clouds of dust tossed up by the horses' hooves, Toria was enchanted by the pastoral scenes they drove past along the route—stone cottages covered with moss emphasizing their age, fragile wooden bridges spanning turbulent brooks, forests silent and deep, and above them the brilliant blue sky with white, puffy clouds moving lazily eastward.

"You'll miss the streets of London after a bit," Sophie commented wryly. "It won't take long for you to grow tired of watching sheep munching in the meadows. Besides, you'll find the nights here are endless—coming early and lasting long."

Stone pillars marked the entrance to the estate, and as the wagons bearing the servants and their baggage rumbled along the gravel road, Toria caught her first glimpse of Sutherland House, the country residence of the Esterbrooks. Constructed of somber gray stone with red slated roofs, its walls ivy clad, it was formal and impressive. Its architecture was Tudor with a jumble of turrets, cupolas, jutting balconies, and a myriad of windows, some mullioned, some of stained glass. Toria imagined that in the wintertime it would be bleak and forbidding, but on a still August afternoon, surrounded by broad velvety lawns and tree-lined avenues and gardens, luxuriant with brilliant beds of flowers, its austere facade was softened, taking on an almost ethereal quality. She soon discovered the house to be a maze of rooms of which probably no member of the family would have been able to make an accurate count.

"Over a hundred, I suppose," the present Marchioness of Esterbrook would say when pressed to give an estimate. "Of course, that's without including corridors, stairways, and hall bedrooms."

"It's even supposed to have a ghost," Sophie whispered with a giggle as they clambered down from the wagons and watched the men unload the luggage. "He lives up in that tall tower which seems to almost touch the sky."

"What fun it will be to explore!" Toria exclaimed.

Mrs. Benedict, who was firmly convinced that country air was bad for her rheumatism, snorted and said sourly, "Small chance you'll have to poke around, with all the things Her Ladyship has scheduled for the next few weeks. The Prince of Wales will be arriving for grouse shooting, and the first day in September she'll sponsor the annual village fair to raise money for the local orphanage. You'll work harder here than you ever did in London, my girl."

If the first few days at Sutherland House were any indication, Mrs. Benedict proved to be absolutely right, for they were spent scouring the countless rooms and corridors, airing the draperies and bedding, and unpacking crates of provisions in preparation for the arrival of the Esterbrooks, to be followed shortly thereafter by their guests.

It was Thursday morning, the day before the arrival of the Prince of Wales, when Lady Clara Esterbrook, returning from a canter through the woods, rang for her maid.

As Toria knelt down to pull off her shiny riding boots, she was surprised to note that her mistress's face was somber and fretful.

"Is something the matter, milady?" she asked anxiously, for normally Lady Clara returned in high spirits from a ride.

"Everything," Lady Clara replied, sailing her black derby across the room in the general direction of the huge four-poster bed. "First off, Piers has arrived with Lord Harrington. As you know, I detest the man. Have you ever seen him? He's come to the town house with Piers several times lately."

"Only from a distance," Toria said, "so I really can't say much about him."

"Well, my brother has informed me that Jamie intends to ask for my hand in marriage, and without a doubt my parents will be ecstatic and say yes without bothering to ask me for my opinion."

Toria frowned, slightly puzzled. "But I thought that was what all debutantes wanted, hoped for, to become betrothed to a member of their class."

Lady Clara's laugh was harsh and humorless. "I rather guess," she said drily, "that I'm the exception. Oh, Toria, I'm not so naïve as to believe that I'd be fortunate enough to fall in love with someone and he with me. I'm realistic and willing to settle for much less, but Jamie is another matter. He follows Piers around like a docile dog. He is silly and vacuous and, worst of all, quite stupid. But as there is no one else in sight eager to marry me, what am I going to do? Even my brother considers it to be a highly satisfactory arrangement, despite the fact that it's perfectly obvious Jamie's attracted not to me but to my money and position."

"No one can force you to marry him." Toria protested.

Lady Clara smiled ruefully. "No, but in the end I imagine I will agree." She removed her riding habit and asked Toria to fetch water for her bath, and next thoroughly confused her maid by saying, "No, don't go. There's something else that has happened equally as bad—possibly even worse. Mother has informed me that I am to sing Saturday night before the Prince of Wales and the other guests. I'll die, I'm certain I will, which might be a good thing, for it would save me from marrying Jamie."

Toria smiled. "Oh, come now," she said brightly. "It won't be as bad as all that. Your voice has been improving steadily. You'll manage."

She was halfway to the door to get the water when Lady Clara flung one last remark over her shoulder. "And besides, I believe I'm coming down with a beastly cold."

As Toria scurried along the dark corridors and steep back stairways leading to the kitchen, she momentarily forgot her mistress and her considerable problems as a picture of Viscount Covington, sitting beside her on a bench near the Serpentine, flashed before her eyes. So he was here, she thought, at last, and somehow, someway, she knew he would manage to meet with her again.

Chapter Eleven

The Prince of Wales arrived on Friday with his en-
tourage, along with thirty other guests accompanied
by their maids and menservants. All of the help was
called upon to perform double duty, and Toria's first
opportunity to observe the house party at close range
was during the lavish tea which was served in the late
afternoon. The women and men, still in their traveling togs, assembled in the drawing room, greeting
each other as if they had not met for many months,
although they had seen each other frequently during
the London season. Toria, dressed in the smart black
uniform she had worn when serving luncheon,
passed platters of scones, cakes, and wafer-thin sandwiches, while the marchioness presided graciously at
the tea table.

Lady Clara was confined to her room with a cold,
and although Toria was aware of Piers's presence as
he moved among the guests, their paths did not
cross. It seemed unbelievable to her that she was in
the presence of the Prince of Wales, who was on
friendly terms with everyone, laughing and chatting
with them as he consumed huge quantities of lobster
salad.

When tea was over, the guests retired to their

rooms to rest and build up energy to tackle the elaborate banquet that was being prepared in the kitchen.

Before dinner Toria stole a minute to peek into the formal dining room and was overawed by its magnificence. A splendid silver epergne, filled with yellow roses, graced the center of the table. The candles in the chandeliers had already been lit, while the footmen in their green and gold livery were standing behind each chair, waiting for the meal to commence. She had a confused impression of sparkling wineglasses and cutlery before slipping away when she heard a murmur of voices in the distance.

Retiring at twelve o'clock, she discovered that every muscle in her body ached. The guests were still up, consuming a lavish supper after an evening of bridge and gossip.

"None of them can go to bed until the prince does," Sophie told her as they wearily climbed the last flight of stairs to their rooms at the top of the house.

"Will it be the same thing all over again tomorrow?" Toria asked in amazement.

Sophie smiled. "Oh, yes and on Sunday too. They won't leave until Monday."

Saturday morning the men departed at an early hour for the shoot, and with their absence the house became relatively quiet—the women content to read or chat as they did their needlework, and later in the day to take leisurely walks through the gardens.

To Toria it began as just another day to live through. The men returned from the shoot thoroughly pleased with the results of their work, having bagged an enormous number of birds. As she passed platters of sandwiches at teatime and listened to the glowing reports of their outing, she shuddered as she wondered how supposedly mature men could gain such pleasure from killing such helpless creatures.

At six o'clock she was summoned to Lady Clara's room to find herself becoming embroiled in a mother and daughter dispute.

"You must sing, Clara," the marchioness was saying in a firm voice as Toria entered.

"How can I," Clara croaked, "when I can barely speak? I should think you could settle for my playing a few pieces on the piano."

Estelle Esterbrook was standing in the center of the room wearing a stunning blue velvet robe trimmed with ermine on the sleeves and collar, wringing her hands in despair.

"Because," she said impatiently, "I promised the prince there would be singing tonight. He'll be expecting some of those sprightly ballads you have learned and be bored to death if you simply drum out a few pieces on the piano. I'm not blaming you, my dear. It isn't your fault you've come down with a cold, but it does place me in a most embarrassing position."

Toria had been standing in the doorway for some time, uncomfortably aware they had completely forgotten her existence. Finally she blurted out, "You rang for me, Lady Clara?"

Clara, who had been gazing moodily out of the window, swung about with an air of triumph. "There is our answer," she declared, pointing a finger at Toria.

"I can't imagine what you are getting at," her mother sputtered.

"Why Toria, of course. She knows all the songs better than I and sings like an angel. I'll accompany her."

"Clara—that's impossible." Lady Estelle's eyes flashed with indignation. "A servant girl singing for the Prince of Wales!"

"And why not? We'll merely introduce her as Miss Victoria Leighton. It's a most impressive name, and if by any chance the prince should discover who she really is, I suspect he'll be highly amused. People are always saying he has such a keen sense of humor."

There was silence in the room as the marchioness began to pace back and forth across the thick carpet. "I can't think of anyone among the guests who could take your place. Lady Hamilton sings, but I doubt she's familiar with your repertoire. Besides, there is no time for her to practice." She ceased her pacing and began to study Toria closely. "Come here," she commanded, and Toria, who was a victim of mixed emotions and on the verge of fleeing from their presence, timidly crossed over to her.

"Why not?" Estelle Esterbrook murmured. "You're right, you know; the prince would consider it amusing. But what will she wear? She can't very well appear as a maid, and I'm certain none of her clothes would be appropriate."

Toria found herself flushing angrily. "I have my Sunday best with me," she said with dignity. "It's a blue silk my aunt made for me. Besides, you haven't asked me how I feel about all this."

"How do you feel, Toria?" Lady Clara asked with a sympathetic smile. "You're quite right. It was very rude of us not to ask for your opinion."

"Scared—scared to death," Toria replied. "But I'll go through with it if it will get you out of a spot."

"Good," the marchioness spoke briskly. "As for a gown, I believe you're about the same size as Baroness Simsbury. We'll let her in on our secret, and knowing Angela, she'll consider it a lark. Now I must hurry and make the arrangements. I'll bring your dress here to Lady Clara's room. You should arrive in the drawing room together. The musicale won't take place much before ten o'clock."

When the marchioness had left, Clara burst out laughing. "What great sport," she exclaimed. "These house parties are usually such a bore, it's fun to have something out of the ordinary happen. You'll be all right, Toria, truly you will. Just pretend we're in the music room singing for Monsieur Etienne. You're not frightened now are you? You've absorbed the shock?"

To her surprise Toria found herself relaxing, joining in with Lady Clara's laughter. "Yes, I'll be all right," she said firmly. "And I agree with you—I think it will be great sport."

They were served a light supper in Lady Clara's suite, and as they ate, Toria's thoughts returned to Piers, as they so often did. She was more excited about singing for him than for the Prince of Wales.

Chapter Twelve

As Toria turned slowly before the long mirror in Lady Clara's bedroom, she decided that Baroness Simsbury's gown was exactly right. It was made of gleaming white satin with a full skirt, and the bodice molded to her slim body emphasized the contour of her firm young breasts. She rejected any jewelry except for a diamond-studded barrette which held her luxuriant hair back from her face.

Lady Clara had chosen to wear a blue tulle gown, and as she searched through her jewel case, selecting a sapphire necklace with matching bracelet, Toria thought she had never appeared more animated, closer to being pretty.

"Toria," she declared, glancing up with a mischievous smile, "this is working out splendidly. Because of my cold, people will have a chance to hear you sing, while I will be spared from making a complete fool of myself. Also, I have obtained a reprieve, be it only a short one, from the boredom of Jamie Harrington's company, for since yesterday I have had a very legitimate excuse to remain cloistered here in my room."

"Do you think he will speak to your parents and ask for your hand in marriage?" Toria asked, anxious to concentrate on any subject but the forthcoming event in the drawing room.

A shadow crossed Lady Clara's face as she sighed deeply. "I expect so, but don't let's worry about that now. With any luck, something might occur between now and Monday morning to prevent it."

"What for instance?"

"Oh, he might be thrown from his horse and break his neck, although that isn't likely, for he's an expert rider. Or perhaps I can be so obnoxious and unpleasant for the balance of the weekend that he will decide that marriage to me, no matter what my monetary worth, would be unbearable."

As she fastened the necklace about her throat, she gave Toria an encouraging smile. "You look extremely lovely. Just right. You'll bring down the house." When Toria did not reply to her comment, she frowned. "You're not still nervous?"

Toria, whose feeling of confidence in her ability to perform had been going up and down like a seesaw, said, "A little."

"We'll remedy that!" Crossing to a table near the window, Lady Clara lifted a decanter of sherry and poured her maid a glass. "Drink this," she commanded. "It's almost time to go downstairs."

As they approached the drawing room, they could hear the rise and fall of many voices, combined with light laughter. Standing in the doorway a step behind Lady Clara, Toria surveyed the scene—the baby grand piano placed near the huge windows that opened on to the terrace, the beautifully gowned ladies, the gentlemen in their formal attire—all seated on small gilt chairs that had been carried down from the ballroom and placed in rows across the room.

The Marchioness of Esterbrook had noted their arrival and, rising from her chair, spoke in a loud, clear voice. Everyone subsided to listen. "As my daughter, Clara, has been fighting a stubborn cold, she is unable to sing tonight, but we are most fortunate to have been able to engage the services of Miss Victoria Leighton. Lady Clara will accompany her."

"Who is Victoria Leighton?" the Prince of Wales asked Lady Estelle, but Clara had already struck a chord on the piano, saving her from giving an answer.

As Toria faced her audience, she saw the Prince of Wales seated between the Marquess and Marchioness of Esterbrook. He's only a rather corpulent, middle-aged gentleman, she told herself sternly, who smokes big fat cigars and eats far too much lobster salad at teatime.

With that she closed her eyes and began to sing as she had never sung before. When she had finished, there was at first complete silence, which to her seemed to stretch endlessly, followed by spontaneous hearty applause as she and Lady Clara took bow after bow.

"You were splendid," Lady Clara whispered, grasping her hand and giving it a warm squeeze.

The Marchioness of Esterbrook had already risen from her chair and was approaching them. "The Prince of Wales wishes to meet you," she said in a low voice and then, noticing the panic on the young girl's face added, "Don't be concerned. You did beautifully, and he was exceedingly impressed with your performance."

With Lady Clara by her side, they drew near to the Prince, dropping deep curtseys as Lady Estelle made the introductions. "You know my daughter, of course," she said in her clipped, cool voice, "and this is Miss Victoria Leighton, who graciously rescued my musicale from disaster."

Summoning enough courage to meet the Prince of Wales's eyes, Toria saw with relief that they were twinkling.

"You have an unusually lovely voice," he said in a deep, sonorous tone. "Tell me, where do you sing?"

Toria gave the marchioness a desperate, frightened look and then, deciding that the truth was preferable to a falsehood, replied calmly, "Sometimes in the scullery, sometimes in the kitchen. I am a servant in this household, Your Highness."

"A servant!" His eyes widened in surprise, followed by an amused chuckle. "Well, you won't be that for very long, my dear, not with such a remarkable voice and splendid appearance."

Lady Estelle's cold fingers clutched Toria's arm, and as she curtseyed and said "Thank you, Your Highness," her mistress broke in quickly, "It was most impressive, sir, wasn't it? But now I think it is time for Miss Leighton to bid us good night."

The Prince of Wales, in the process of lighting a cigar, raised a hand in protest. "But my dear Estelle," he said, "it seems clear to me Miss Leighton is entitled to at least a glass of champagne, if not supper at midnight to celebrate her success. Will midnight be too late for you, Cinderella?" he finished with a smile.

"Midnight, sir, would be far too late," she replied.

"Well, at least champagne?" he asked, and she

nodded her head in agreement, despite the fact that she sensed the Marchioness of Esterbrook's disapproval, for after all, she thought defiantly, didn't she deserve some slight reward for skillfully pulling her employer's chestnuts out of the fire.

The Marquess of Esterbrook, who up until now had not uttered one word, cleared his throat loudly and muttered, "Without a doubt champagne is in order."

A footman bearing a silver tray appeared miraculously, and the prince beckoned to Toria to sit beside him in the chair previously occupied by the marchioness.

Taking a glass from the tray, she sipped the sparkling liquid cautiously. "I've never tasted champagne before," she admitted.

"It makes some people sneeze and others woozy," the Prince of Wales remarked, his eyes fastened on her face as he spoke. "By the way, I once knew a lady remarkably like you—her name was Letty Leighton. Are you by any chance related?"

"She was my mother," Toria replied gravely.

"Was?"

"Yes, she died at my birth."

"And your father, who was he?" the Prince asked.

"I never knew him, sir."

The Prince of Wales finished his champagne and rose laboriously to his feet. "What a tragedy!" He spoke softly and with a bow of his head indicated that the interview was over.

As he watched her depart, he turned to the Duke of Blakesley, who was standing behind him. "Strange," he said, "I haven't thought of Letty Leighton in years. You know how the lives of these

74

actresses are—like a comet they streak across the sky and disappear. I hadn't the least idea she had died and before doing so gave birth to a daughter so similar in appearance that it's immensely disturbing."

"I've seen the daughter somewhere before." Alex was frowning thoughtfully, attempting yet failing to pinpoint the incident. "It's a face you'd never forget."

Agreeing, the prince smiled at his hostess. "I'm ready for that game of bridge, Estelle, so sharpen your wits. You're joining us, Alex?" And as the duke agreed, they followed the other guests to the library and card room, where tables had already been set up.

Toria left the drawing room and was crossing the hallway in the direction of the back stairs, reluctant to have her moment of glory over, when someone touched her shoulder, and swinging about, she saw that it was Piers. All during her conversation with the prince, she had been aware of his presence in the background, observing the unusual scene.

"Rendezvous with me tonight, Toria," he whispered urgently. "At twelve o'clock, in the rose garden by the marble fountain."

Slowly she shook her head. "No," she replied. "It would be foolhardy for me to do so."

"There'll be no danger of discovery," he reassured her. "By then they'll be so intent on their dreary game of bridge and so besotted by brandy that no one will have the slightest suspicion of our meeting. Please, I must speak with you. I'll be there, waiting, whether you are or not."

Before she could protest he was gone, and she watched him leave the drawing room with his sister and a young man who she knew must be Lord Harrington. With a sigh she placed her empty champagne glass on a table and moved in the direction of the back stairway and her bedroom. A Cinderella, she thought despairingly, with no chance at all to marry her prince.

Chapter Thirteen

Her room on the top floor of Sutherland House appeared even smaller and dingier when she returned to it that night, a stark contrast to the dazzling scene she had witnessed such a short time ago, a grim reminder that she was isolated in one world and Piers in another, with no way to bridge the gap.

As she carefully removed the white satin gown, her thoughts were not of the highly favorable reaction her performance had received but of Piers and his urgent request. In her own mind she hadn't accepted or rejected it, and slipping into a cotton robe, she began to pace back and forth from the window to the door—still indecisive, torn between a burning desire to be with him once more and the sobering knowledge that if his demands became importunate, she might very well find herself conceding, swept away on a wave of emotion that would become irresistible.

Certainly that afternoon in Hyde Park had taught her that he had the power to touch a chord deep inside her that had never been touched before.

She knew instinctively that to meet outside in the moonlight would be a step fraught with danger. But eventually the craving to see him again won out over caution, and at midnight she changed into her blue silk dress, throwing her dark cape about her shoulders as on tiptoe she descended the stairs.

She encountered no one on the way. It was a still, warm August night—the sky cloudless, the full moon silvering the path that led to the formal gardens. When she approached the rose garden, she saw that he was already there. The only sound that broke the silence of the night was the gentle splash of the water in the marble fountain and the hoarse croak of a frog in a nearby pond.

He heard her footsteps on the brick path and, swinging around, gave a triumphant laugh. "You decided to come—how marvelous!"

She could see his face quite clearly in the moonlight, his brilliant blue eyes, which had the power to cast a spell over her. He had never appeared more handsome, more debonair.

"I shouldn't have come," she replied. Her voice shook, and she bit her lower lip, angry at herself for showing so clearly how easily he could shatter her composure.

"And not give me the opportunity to tell you how magnificent you were this evening? I applauded you vigorously with the others. I applauded you silently too when I saw how cleverly you managed your meeting with the prince."

"Not so cleverly," she said ruefully. "I simply told the truth. It was fortunate he responded the way he did, although I fear your mother did not appreciate the manner in which I handled the situation."

"Nonsense! She's very pleased. She's even reached the stage where she believes she is entirely responsible for a very adroit coup, despite the fact it was

Clara's idea originally. How many hostesses can amuse the Prince of Wales with such a charming episode?"

"I'm beginning to feel somewhat like a court jester."

"They went out of style long ago. You are you—a most unusual person. But surely you are aware I didn't ask you to meet me here tonight merely to talk?"

He moved close to her and, cupping her chin in his hand, slowly turned her face upward until every beautiful feature was outlined in the moonlight.

Her success as a singer, the kind words of the prince, the candlelight, the champagne, the applause, and now his touch, all conspired to set her mind in a whirl. She felt as if she were in the center of a kaleidoscope, spinning around and around, so when he gathered her in his arms, she offered no resistance, responding to his passionate kiss with equal passion.

"You are a minx," he murmured, "an adorable minx." He drew her to a stone bench near the fountain and, still holding her close to him, stroked her soft golden hair, removing the diamond barrette so that her curls spilled about her face and down to her shoulders. He kissed her again, this time tenderly as if she were made of fragile china and might break. "Will you leave your door unlocked tonight, Toria?" he asked urgently.

She was not surprised by his request, for despite her innocence, her naïveté, she had known all along that eventually he would ask that question. She was amazed to discover that she wanted this evening to end as he wanted it to end—locked in each other's arms.

She drew away from him a little, in time to see a look of triumph spread across his face. The warnings of Mrs. Benedict returned like homing pigeons. After tonight, what? she thought, and suddenly the moon became not a warm lovers' moon but cold and remote. She was no longer weak and compliant, but determined to resist his demands.

"No," she said stiffly. "If I've misled you, I'm sorry, but I can't."

His heavy brows rose, registering his surprise, revealing all too clearly that he was not accustomed to rejection. If he failed in his pursuit of her tonight, he would be even more determined to eventually win out. I will not be like my mother, she told herself sternly, and rising from the bench she gave him a clipped "Good night."

As she ran along the garden path toward the lighted mansion, which stood like a shimmering jewel before her, she was thankful he made no effort to follow. If he had attempted to fold her in his arms again, she was quite certain her resistance would have crumbled and her answer would have been yes.

Lord Blakesley, who had been grateful to make his escape from the bridge table, was walking slowly up and down a garden path at Sutherland House, enjoying a cool breeze and a cigarette, when he heard hurrying footsteps coming from the direction of the rose garden. Before he could step off the path, the figure of a young girl stumbled against him and would have fallen to the ground if he had not reached out and caught her in time.

"Steady now," he said easily, and as the hood of her cape fell back and the moonlight outlined her face, he recognized the servant girl who had sung for them so beautifully earlier in the evening. Her face was streaked with tears and she was breathing heavily. "Do you need a strong arm to protect you?" he asked.

Proudly she stood erect and wiped her wet cheeks quickly with her hands. "No, thank you," she replied, struggling to recover her poise. "I can take care of myself."

He gave a triumphant laugh, for her words brought back in a flash that night several months ago at the Alhambra when Dickie Hadley would have attempted to add her to his list of conquests if he had not intervened. "I believe," he said in amusement, "that I heard you make the same statement once before, outside the Alhambra." It's probably that rascal Piers who has upset her so, Alex silently concluded, clenching and unclenching his hands in anger. Piers is up to mischief again, unable to resist the charms of an attractive servant girl.

Toria was smiling now, her tears temporarily forgotten, acknowledging his presence with a graceful curtsey. "I remember you too." She almost whispered the words. "Thank you for offering to come to my rescue again, but there's no need, as I'm perfectly all right." With a dip of her golden head she departed, leaving him to listen to her light steps fading away as he toyed with the idea of seeking out young Piers to give him a thorough dressing down.

Finally deciding that delivering a lecture to the viscount would accomplish nothing, he discarded his cigarette, returning reluctantly to the smoke-filled, brightly lit card room.

The game was still in progress, and as he crossed to a table at the far end of the room where his fiancée,

Lady Caroline Stanley, was seated, he felt a sudden desire to grasp her by the hand and carry her away with him into the garden. But he dismissed the thought as soon as it was born, for it was obvious that she was completely immersed in the game. Besides, he knew she would resist such a request, saying in her cool, even voice, "Don't be tiresome, darling."

He studied her carefully. She was certainly a magnificent woman—poised, exquisitely groomed, a honey blond with the chiseled features of an aristocrat. He had known her since childhood. His parents and hers had assumed from the beginning that eventually they would marry, considering it a perfect solution to join together two of the great houses in England. There had never been any doubt in his mind that as the Duchess of Blakesley she would fulfill all the requirements of her high position. Nevertheless, lately he had become depressed thinking about their relationship, and now tonight, after his brief encounter in the moonlight with Toria Leighton, he felt a sharp twinge of regret that Lady Caroline lacked one quality which the young servant girl seemed to possess in abundance—ardor and passion.

The last hand had been played and the servants were passing trays of champagne along with a cold collation. Moving toward Lady Caroline, Alex touched her smooth white shoulders caressingly as he whispered softly so that she alone could hear, "It's such a lovely night, Caroline. Let's take a stroll in the garden."

She delicately stifled a yawn. "It's far too late, darling," she replied. "Besides I'm weary and wish to retire."

With a sigh he accepted a glass of champagne from

a waiter, and as he sipped the cool liquid, he began to wonder if his future wife, who never failed in the presence of others to be completely self-controlled and self-contained, would prove to be the same in the bedroom. With an ironic smile, he granted that this question could not be resolved until after the wedding, although he was beginning to suspect that Lady Caroline, despite the fact she would dutifully agree to bear his children, would be as frigid in bed as the tip of an iceberg.

Chapter Fourteen

The servants in Sutherland House had barely recovered from their arduous duties during the long country weekend when they were swept into another whirlwind of activity as the Marchioness of Esterbrook laid plans for the fair that she sponsored each September on the grounds of the estate.

Soon the lawns surrounding the manor house were inundated with workmen setting up booths covered by gay striped awnings. Women from the village began to arrive to stock the shelves with all sorts of articles they had made during the long winter months. Cakes and other mouth-watering foods were also to be put on display, while a variety of games were planned for the children. There was a booth where lemonade was to be served and a round wooden dance floor was erected for dancing.

"People come from far and near," Mrs. Benedict explained to Toria. "It's the one time during the year when the gentry consent to mingle with us ordinary folk."

At the beginning of the week, it was cloudy and windy, giving cause for some concern, but on Saturday, the day the fair was to commence, the skies miraculously cleared, giving a promise of fine weather.

"Queen's weather," Mrs. Benedict predicted solemnly at breakfast that morning. "I can't remember ever seeing a drop of rain on the day of the Marchioness's fair."

Toria and Sophie were put in charge of the lemonade stand and were kept busy supplying the needs of the throngs of thirsty spectators. It wasn't until late in the afternoon that they were given some free time to stroll about the grounds, discarding their caps and voluminous aprons, mingling with the crowds of jostling, laughing villagers and the gentry from surrounding estates.

"I don't feel like a servant, do you?" Sophie whispered. Toria, who was wearing her blue silk dress with a blue velvet ribbon tying back her hair, agreed that she didn't either. For the first time since her last meeting with Viscount Covington in the rose garden, she began to look about her with interest, to feel lighthearted and almost gay.

"Will you be dancing tonight?" Toria asked her friend.

Sophie nodded her head vigorously. "Oh, yes indeed. I want you to meet Ralph. You'll find the band from the village very good, and don't worry, for you'll have so many partners, there'll be little time to catch your breath."

Toria, barely listening, had been searching among the crowd for Piers. At last she spotted him strolling leisurely some distance ahead of them, his arm casually linking the arm of a lady dressed in a pale pink muslin gown, holding a pink ruffled parasol over her head.

"Who is that?" she asked Sophie.

"Where?" Sophie, her thoughts still occupied with the pleasures that the night ahead would hold, emerged from a delightful trance.

"The woman with Lord Covington."

"Oh, that's Lady Charlotte Middleton. Her father has an estate in the next township. Many believe the viscount intends to marry her. It's certain anyway that his parents are anxious to see them wed."

Toria felt her high spirits plummet. "Is she very lovely?" she questioned. "We're not close enough for me to tell."

"Tolerably so. No great beauty, but pretty enough. Why do you ask?"

"No reason really. I guess I'm as curious as the rest of the staff about the Esterbrooks. Now, take Lady Clara, for instance. She's ahead of us, walking as far away from Lord Harrington as she possibly can. It's easy to see why she dislikes him so. Have you ever heard his high-pitched giggle? It's mortifying to hear. I suppose in the long run she'll be forced to become betrothed to him, whether she wants to or not."

"I understand he's already asked for her hand and she has refused him, much to her parents' displeasure."

"So that's why she has been so disconsolate lately," Toria said. Ever since the night she had sung for the Prince of Wales, Lady Clara had become distant and evasive, spending long hours in the saddle and answering Toria's questions with a curt "yes" or "no."

"Oh, eventually she'll be forced to agree," Sophie

predicted. "Have you seen any other suitor on the horizon?"

They had drawn close to Lady Charlotte and the viscount, and when he saw them, he called out, "Be sure not to miss the dance tonight and save at least one for me." He addressed his remarks to both of them, but his eyes were on Toria's face, and she blushed, not answering him or meeting his gaze.

"Really, Piers," his companion said in a high, clear voice. "Surely you don't intend to dance with the servants or the village girls?"

"I always do," he replied, "on the night of my mother's fair."

"But not with me, you won't!" Toria muttered fiercely under her breath.

Sophie stared at her in astonishment. "Whyever not?" she burst out. "He only meant to be gracious."

"Gracious! I considered him patronizing."

They continued their stroll in silence, Sophie darting anxious glances at her friend from time to time as Toria, with a great effort, started to exclaim over the needlepoint collection the vicar's wife had on display. She was relieved when it was time to return to the kitchen for an early supper and that Sophie, caught up in the excitement of discussing the evening ahead, seemed to have forgotten the subject of Viscount Covington.

Later, when the dancing commenced, Toria stood in the shadows watching the colorful scene—the musicians in their scarlet coats, the area around them aglow with Chinese lanterns that had been strung in the trees. She was not alone for long, for soon one of the footman, seeing her standing there, grasped her hand, pulling her onto the polished floor.

Not until after a series of gavottes, mazurkas, and carefree country dances did the musicians play a slow, haunting valse, and she found herself in the arms of Viscount Covington.

They did not exchange a word, but as they circled around and around the floor, their eyes met and held, creating an atmosphere of excitement between them that could not be denied. Toria knew that any words uttered at that moment would have been superfluous and meaningless, for his glance was telling her all that she needed to know, that despite the vast differences in their backgrounds, despite their opposite stations in life, she fascinated him, and he was falling in love with her. Of course, she had known for some time that she was in love with him.

Love—the magical word that cannot be defined. It defies description, but when it exists between a man and a woman it is like a lyrical poem or a marvelous piece of music, born to be enjoyed exactly as it is, without analysis or dissection.

The last note of the violins slowly died, and someone broke the silence enveloping them by announcing that refreshments were being served in the great hall. As the dancers and spectators drifted across the lawns toward the manor house, Piers, without a word, encircled her slender waist and guided her toward the rose garden, to the stone bench by the marble fountain.

"Don't say a word," he whispered when she opened her lips to protest. "I have rehearsed a speech, and nothing in this world will prevent me from delivering it. It's very brief." He drew her to him. She did not resist. "Only three words—the oldest, most enduring words ever spoken—I love you."

She raised her hands in a graceful, hopeless gesture.

"I know," he said with an endearing smile, "exactly what you intend to say, but let me tell you this—you are wrong if you think I am going to ask you to be mine without benefit of wedlock. You will never imagine the torment I have gone through these past few days, ever since you deserted me here in this very spot. I want you Toria. Will you marry me?"

"Marry!" she exclaimed in astonishment. "You must be bewitched by the moonlight, milord. Lords never marry servant girls."

"Then it's time one did and broke an outmoded tradition."

"How would you explain such an occurrence to your parents?"

He sat beside her, making no attempt to touch her. "What could they do, faced with a fait accompli?" he asked. "I am their only son. I doubt very much if they would have the courage to disinherit me. And you, my darling Toria, are fully capable of rising to the challenge. I could search every nook and cranny of England and fail to find anyone more beautiful, more fascinating than you. If not an aristocrat by birth, you possess all the ingredients to become one. Oh, for a while there would be a certain amount of gossip among the so-called elite, who do not enjoy seeing their bastions breached, but soon it would be forgotten. You would not only be accepted but welcomed as a member of our inner circle."

"You must be mad!" she exclaimed.

"Not mad—hopelessly in love." He pulled her gently to him, and as he kissed her deeply, he stroked her golden hair.

"Now listen carefully to me," he said, drawing away from her with a great effort. "Tonight is not our night for a romantic interlude, much as I crave it. It is the night to lay meticulous plans, and if you follow my instructions to the letter, I promise you that although there will be stormy days ahead, the storm will eventually pass, as all storms do, and we will be rewarded with an idyllic life together.

"Next Thursday you must confront the awe-inspiring Mrs. Stackhouse and, with tears in those lovely eyes, tell her that some member of your family is at death's door. Beg for a few days to travel to London. I am certain she will grant it. I've discovered over the years that she is not made of stone. She does have some compassion.

"I wager she will even arrange to have one of the grooms drive you to Winston station, where you will board the train for London, debarking at the next stop, where I will be waiting for you.

"By then, I will have made all the arrangements down to the minutest detail—what justice of the peace will marry us, where we will spend our brief but glorious honeymoon. On Monday you will return to Winston and thank Mrs. Stackhouse politely for her kindness, and when the moment seems propitious, I will inform my illustrious parents that I am a happily married man and intend to remain so."

They heard voices in the distance—another couple seeking the privacy of the rose garden—and quickly he grasped her hand and led her to the protection of a grove of beech trees.

In the shadows he drew her to him once more and whispered fiercely, "Give me your answer, Toria— yes or no?"

"Oh, yes, yes," she whispered back. "I'll do exactly as you say, for I love you, Piers. I too have been miserable lately, and now miraculously I am caught up in such a wave of happiness, I can hardly bear it. Do you suppose I could be dreaming?"

He laughed. "It is no dream, my darling. This Friday night you will be mine, I will be yours, and no one, nothing will have the power to change the direction of our lives." He kissed her once more and pressed a ring into her hand. "Wear this around your neck as a symbol of my commitment. But now you must go. It would be disastrous if anyone suspected we had been together."

Hand in hand, they left the shelter of the beech grove. "Return to the house," he instructed her. "Enjoy your supper—I'll follow along afterwards."

Before hiding the ring in her pocket, she examined it with wonder and delight. It was fashioned in exquisite gold encircled with tiny diamonds. She had never seen anything more lovely in all her life.

In a delightful trance she sped across the lawns, past the deserted dance floor, past the empty booths and entered the great hall, losing herself in the crowd.

As she joined Sophie and some of the other servants at one of the long tables, she was breathing heavily, and Sophie gave her a sharp look. "Where have you been?" she asked.

"Lady Clara had need of my services."

"They never allow us one free night," Sophie complained. "Without us they would be completely helpless."

Toria saw Piers enter the hall and go directly to the table where Lady Charlotte Middleton was seated. She felt a sharp stab of jealously until she realized that she should no longer be jealous of Lady Charlotte or anyone else. For he would soon be hers. She thought her heart would burst, it was filled with such great joy.

That night she could not sleep, fearful that if she did, she would awaken to discover that her meeting with Piers in the rose garden had been a dream, fading into nothingness as all dreams are wont to do in the morning light.

Chapter Fifteen

On Thursday morning Toria mustered enough courage to approach Mrs. Stackhouse, who was working on her accounts in her small office off the kitchen.

"I was wondering, Mrs. Stackhouse," she began in a tremulous voice, "if I might have a few days off."

"A few days off!" Mrs. Stackhouse's eyebrows rose heavenward in surprise. "Surely you've been with us long enough, my girl, to know we don't give days off except under very unusual circumstances."

"But this is unusual, Mrs. Stackhouse," Toria plunged onward. "My grandfather in London is desperately ill. I just received word of it in the morning post. You see, he's the only close relative I have with the exception of my aunt."

The housekeeper tapped her fingers briskly on the top of her desk, giving Toria a shrewd glance. "In that case," she said reluctantly, "it might be arranged. You're a hard worker, and I must confess it came to me as a surprise. At the beginning I considered you far too pretty and undernourished to be much help to me. When would you want to go?"

"Tomorrow, if possible, and I'd return on Monday, no matter what."

"All right. I wouldn't want it to be on my conscience if he should die and I had refused you. I'll see that you get a ride to the station in the morning. Now be off with you and work doubly hard today and this evening to make up for lost time."

She returned to her accounts with a scowl, and Toria, unable to believe her good fortune, hurried back to her tasks, remembering to keep a suitable expression of sorrow and distress on her face.

She was driven to the station early the next morning by one of the grooms, who was picking up supplies in the village. In a daze she climbed aboard the London train, carrying a valise with her pitiful collection of clothing, wearing her blue silk dress and a plain straw bonnet—its only decoration a blue velvet ribbon tied under her chin.

It was a thirty minute ride to the next stop, and when she stepped onto the station platform, her heart sank when she caught no sight of Viscount Covington. A few passengers brushed by her, and as the train moved onward, puffing, panting, and ejecting great clouds of steam, she was alone on the platform, except for the ticket agent who peered at her curiously through his small grilled window.

Avoiding his gaze, she sat down on a wooden bench, and, as the minutes ticked slowly by with no sign of Piers, she began to imagine that all sorts of dreadful events might have occurred—an accident on the road, perhaps, or maybe he had changed his mind about marrying her and lacked the courage to tell her so.

After endless hours of waiting, she lost track of the time, but eventually she was forced to concede that Piers, for some reason or another, had failed to keep his promise. It was hot and uncomfortable sitting in

94

the blazing sunlight on a hard wooden bench, so when a train pulled into the station, she boarded it to make the return trip to the village of Winston. As no one was there to meet her, she was forced to walk on foot to Sutherland House, reaching her destination in the early evening, famished and exhausted.

Explaining to the surprised Mrs. Stackhouse that as she had found her grandfather in a coma which might last for weeks she saw no reason to linger in London, she joined the servants at the supper table. Despite her turbulent emotions, she discovered she was ravenous. She had no sooner finished her meal than Lady Clara's bell started to ring, and hurrying to Her Ladyship's room, she entered an atmosphere of disarray.

"Thank heavens you have returned," Lady Clara exclaimed. "The maid who took your place today hadn't the slightest notion of how to dress my hair, and worst of all, my bath water was tepid." Glancing at Toria's distraught face, she added hurriedly, "I'm sorry about the illness in your family, Toria. Is your grandfather any better? He must be for you to come back so soon."

"He was in a coma, milady, and as the doctor predicted it could last for weeks, perhaps months, I saw no reason to stay." Toria disliked herself for telling such a bald-faced lie. "Now let's see how I can improve the arrangement of your hair," she added, to change the topic of conversation.

Lady Clara sat in front of her dressing table, her eyes following Toria's skillful fingers as she worked with brush and comb. "I'm aware I have been difficult lately," she confessed, "but you can't imagine how dreadful it is to be constantly feuding with your parents. They still refuse to accept my rejection of Lord Harrington. In fact, against my wishes they've actually asked him here for the weekend. Every time I turn around he will be close beside me. Bulldog determination is one quality he does possess."

"It must be a great strain on your nerves," Toria commiserated soothingly, "but if you continue to say no, what can they do? I cannot imagine them dragging you to the altar."

Despite her somber mood, Lady Clara found herself laughing. "You are a tonic, Toria. How I've missed you. All in all, it's been a terrible day, with my brother, Piers, engaging in a dreadful row with my father before storming out of the house and taking off for London."

Toria's body tensed. She took a deep breath before asking in a cool, detached manner. "Whatever caused the argument?"

Her mistress sighed deeply. "Oh, it's something that's been brewing for a long time. My parents have been attempting without success to persuade Piers to marry Lady Charlotte Middleton. Today my father abandoned his conciliatory tactics and issued an ultimatum—either marry Lady Charlotte, he told my brother, or face disinheritance."

"What will be the outcome?" Toria asked, her hands beginning to tremble.

Lady Clara shrugged her shoulders with nonchalance. "Who knows? He's always been carefree and unreliable—quite the scamp. Lately he's been preoccupied with another love affair. I can always tell. I wonder what poor girl he's been hoodwinking this time?"

Toria felt terror strike her heart. "Whatever do you mean, milady?"

"Oh, it's always very apparent when he's stalking his prey. There's a certain expression of triumph in his eyes which is thoroughly degrading. I am certain that this morning when he informed my parents he was going hunting with some officers in his regiment, he was going hunting all right, but after a pretty skirt rather than a fox. My parents sensed it too—hence the unpleasant session in the library."

Toria felt the room spinning around her and grasped the back of Lady Clara's chair to prevent herself from falling.

"What's the matter, Toria?" Lady Clara asked sharply. "Suddenly you have become very pale and your hands are shaking."

"Oh, it's nothing, nothing," Toria responded quickly. "It was a long, tiring trip today, and also I suppose I was surprised at the low opinion you hold of your brother."

Lady Clara laughed. "Oh, we're the best of friends. I don't begrudge him his affairs—in fact, if anything, I think I envy him a little. Besides, he's no better or worse than the other officers in his regiment. It's a matter of pride with them to try to outmatch each other by proving to be the greatest rake. I wouldn't be the least surprised if right at this very moment he is discussing his latest escapade in minute detail at The Guards in London."

Toria blushed a fiery red. Was it possible that Piers' avowal of undying love and his wedding plans had been merely a ruse? That he had no intention of marriage, being convinced that once they were alone he would have his way with her?

Every fiber in her body rejected such a supposition. Surely he was capable of loving sincerely, and although she was not so stupid as to believe she was the first woman in his life, she refused to accept his sister's opinion of his complete lack of character.

The ring he had given her felt cold against her warm body. It was her talisman, her proof that he was faithful, and as she watched Lady Clara give her coiffure a final pat of approval, Toria decided that she had only one course to follow—to continue believing in Piers and to wait patiently for him to return with a logical explanation.

Chapter Sixteen

It was the first week in October, and the activity at Sutherland House had reached a crescendo as plans for the trek back to London for the Little Season were set in motion.

It was also more than three weeks since Toria had returned from her aborted rendezvous with Viscount Covington. Since then she had not caught a glimpse of him, and although he had warned her of the necessity of being circumspect, nevertheless she had hoped he would manage to seek her out, if only by a look to reassure her of his love. But as far as she knew, he had failed to put in an appearance at Sutherland House, and as Lady Clara had become silent regarding the outcome of the argument with his father, Toria remained in the dark, not knowing the present status of their relationship. As the days dragged by, she found it more and more difficult to continue to have faith in him.

It was the day before their departure for London. The servants were gathered around the long table in the kitchen at supper, with Mrs. Stackhouse presiding, when Lucy, the Marchioness of Esterbrook's personal maid, arrived breathless and in a high state of excitement. "Have you heard the great news about the betrothal?" she exclaimed.

"You mean Lady Clara has finally consented to marry Lord Harrington?" Toria inquired.

"Oh, no—Viscount Covington has asked for Lady Charlotte's hand in marriage, and she has accepted him."

"But that can't be!" Toria cried out as everyone at the table turned to stare at her in amazement.

"What do you mean it can't be?" Mrs. Stackhouse asked forcefully.

"I meant, I only meant," Toria stammered, "that I've been led to believe he wasn't the marrying kind."

"He wasn't," Mrs. Stackhouse replied succinctly. "But sooner or later most of these young bloods settle down. However, it doesn't follow that he won't continue to have his flings on the side. I don't envy Lady Charlotte her position."

"As far as we're concerned, it means only all kinds of parties and extra work," Sophie said dolefully. "I for one will be happy when it's over and he's set up in his own establishment."

Dazedly Toria heard the conversation swirl about her as if from a great distance, as each of the servants added his or her contribution to the subject of the viscount's approaching marriage.

Toria sat there, her supper untouched, totally unable to absorb the horrendous news. It just can't be, she kept reassuring herself over and over again. There's been some dreadful mistake.

Instinctively her fingers found the diamond ring which was concealed under her uniform, as if touching it would prove that Lucy had been mistaken and had misinterpreted what she had overheard.

100

"Lady Estelle is ecstatic," Lucy prattled on, pleased to be the bearer of such a fascinating announcement. "She told the Marquess only this afternoon that Lady Charlotte's parents are planning a huge wedding at St. Margaret's—six attendants, I believe, with a flower girl and a ring bearer, with a reception following at their town house in Belgrave Square."

"Well, at least we won't be involved in that," Mrs. Stackhouse remarked with a sigh of relief. "We'll have enough on our hands when Lady Clara marries, which I expect will be soon." Standing up quickly, she gave the signal that the time for dallying had ended and it was back to work for the entire staff.

Toria's one overpowering desire was to escape to her room, where she could be alone and try to make some sense out of Lucy's announcement. But it was not to be, for as she was leaving the kitchen, Lady Clara's bell clanged, summoning her to report for duty.

Then she recalled that there was a ball scheduled for that night at a nearby estate, which meant at least an hour of work assisting Lady Clara in her preparations. Usually she looked forward to this time, enjoying helping her mistress into one of her splendid gowns, watching her as she opened her jewel box and made the important decision of whether to wear her diamonds, her pearls, or the ruby pendant her parents had presented to her at Christmas.

But tonight as Toria climbed the stairs to Lady Clara's suite, she was trembling from head to foot, unable to imagine how she could remain calm for the next hour or two, how she could possibly preserve her dignity so that no one would suspect she was crushed and bewildered by the conversation in the kitchen.

As she entered Lady Clara's bedroom, she could tell by the expression on her mistress's face that it was true—something unusual had occurred in the household.

"Piers is betrothed, Toria," she began without preamble. "We believed he was in London all this time, but instead of that, he has been a guest of the Middletons. He and Lady Charlotte drove over this afternoon to inform my parents of their engagement before the announcement appears in the papers. Isn't it exciting? It's high time my brother marries, for he's past twenty-one. But best of all, it will spare me for awhile from making a decision about Lord Harrington. One wedding at a time will be quite enough to keep my mother occupied."

Toria, on the brink of bursting out, "How can he marry her when he is pledged to me?" caught herself from making the remark, astute enough to realize, despite the bitter blow she had received, that although she and Lady Clara had established an unusually close friendship, nonetheless her mistress was a member of the aristocracy, and her reaction to such a disclosure would be vehemently on her brother's side. Servant girls simply did not become betrothed to members of the nobility. She would conclude that Toria had lost her senses.

With supreme effort, she went about her tasks—calm on the surface, agreeing with Lady Clara that undoubtedly the question of her marriage to Lord Harrington would be postponed.

As she dressed her mistress's hair, she glanced at her own image in the mirror and was amazed that she appeared composed, serene, politely interested in what Lady Clara was saying.

It wasn't until Lady Clara was ready to leave for the ball and Toria was adjusting her ermine cape about her shoulders, that she was struck by the horrible, irrefutable fact that she did not have a shred of proof of the viscount's proposal, for of what consequence would a gold ring sprinkled with diamonds be?

As Lady Clara smiled at her and waved her hand in farewell, Toria responded automatically with a smile and a nod, accepting at last the stark, cold fact that Viscount Covington had never really intended to make her his bride.

Chapter Seventeen

"You fool," Sophie burst out. "To be so naïve as to believe a viscount would contemplate marriage to a servant girl!"

After Lady Clara had departed for the ball, Toria, her duties temporarily over, had fled to her room and, throwing herself on the bed, had allowed her tears to flow freely. Sophie had overheard her weeping, and when she tapped lightly on the door and entered, her first question was, "Toria, what on earth is the matter?"

Toria, who felt she must unburden her heart to someone, had spilled out the entire story.

"I thought he loved me," Toria sobbed.

"Love—he doesn't know the meaning of the word," exclaimed Sophie. "It was only a clever ruse to seduce you. He might even have planned a mock marriage to lull your suspicions. All along I have thought you were far too smart, Toria, to be taken in by such a wastrel. Don't you realize that after a few days with you, it would have been the end, as far as he was concerned? And if you had become with child he wouldn't have lifted one finger to rescue you from your predicament. You're most fortunate he changed his mind and failed to meet you."

"He gave me this ring," Toria said, slipping it off from its chain and showing it to Sophie.

"What does a diamond ring mean to a man of great property?" Sophie sputtered. "It was simply another inducement to encourage you to run away with him."

"Yet I'm still puzzled as to why he didn't follow through with his plan."

Sophie laughed harshly. "Well, it's clear as a bell to me and would be clear to you too if you listened to the gossip below stairs. When faced with strong opposition, the viscount is as weak as a kitten. Do you think he would have the courage to risk being disinherited for a few nights in bed with a servant girl—no matter how fascinating he might consider her to be? It's all very simple, my dear Toria. His father gave him an ultimatum—marry Lady Charlotte or else. He protested at the outset, fumed at his club for a few days, but his decision was inevitable, and in the end he consented to follow his parents' wishes. But after the honeymoon is over, it wouldn't surprise me in the least if he continues his pursuit of you, giving all sorts of trumped-up excuses as to why he was forced to the altar despite his enduring love."

"I will never give him that opportunity," Toria declared proudly.

Puzzled, Sophie watched as Toria reached for her woolen cape and wrapped it about her. "Where are you going?" she demanded, frightened by the wooden expression on her friend's face.

"Don't worry," Toria said with a bitter laugh. "I'm going to the rose garden, but I have no intention of throwing myself into the pond."

She was clutching the diamond ring in her hand,

studying it with the deepest aversion. "I am about to throw this thing into the marble fountain," she continued, "and I will stay there watching until it sinks to the bottom. And I will make myself a pledge never, for as long as I live, to love or trust another man. I will also make a vow that some day Viscount Covington will pay dearly for his deception!"

Chapter Eighteen

Upon her return to London, Toria Leighton found her position as a lady's maid in the town house of the Marquess of Esterbrook untenable. The constant downstairs gossip and speculation about the viscount's approaching marriage became increasingly painful for her to bear, and slowly a plan for her future began to evolve in her mind.

She was young, and enough people had told her that she was beautiful to convince her it was true; in addition, she had a voice that was apparently sufficiently pleasing to satisfy even the Prince of Wales. The burning question, therefore, was how to intelligently capitalize on her attributes.

On the day before the marriage of Viscount Covington, she packed her valise, and as excitement was running at a high pitch in the household, her departure passed unnoticed. She left with less than four pounds in her pocket. Not even Sophie, her closest friend, was aware she had gone until Lady Clara rang for Toria to attend her while dressing for the prenuptial dinner. There was some consternation as to where Lady Clara's personal maid could have gone, but no one could come up with even one clue as to why she had vanished.

Rejecting the idea of returning to her grandfather's house, she found that her immediate problem was where to spend the night. She was fortunate to rent a room in a run-down boardinghouse in Honey Lane off Cheapside.

She had already given a great deal of thought to what her next step would be, early on ruling out the prospect of employment at Lucille's or Worth's, convinced that constant subservience to their clientele would be as distasteful as slaving in some nobleman's establishment.

Admitting that her options were limited and that in order to survive she must find work immediately, the next morning she paid a visit to the Alhambra.

Her first view of the theater in Leicester Square by daylight was a disappointment. She remembered it after darkness had fallen, at night, when it had taken on an aura of glamour, a certain fairlike quality. But today it seemed shabby, a trifle seedy, its facade far too ornate and brash.

The doorman, a lean, cantankerous individual with a perpetual scowl on his face, looked up from the sporting pages of his newspaper when she approached him, and curtly refused her entry.

"But I have an appointment with the manager," she protested, attempting to impress him by a haughty toss of her head. He still refused to admit her, returning to his newspaper and ignoring her desperate plea to please make an exception in her case and let her pass.

She was on the verge of leaving, her bravado utterly destroyed, when a jocular voice behind her said, "Wait a minute, young miss. Why do you wish to see the manager?" Swinging about, she confronted the strangest individual she had ever encountered. He was a corpulent man, well past middle age, wearing a long velvet cape lined with brown, glossy fur. His black, wide-brimmed hat was pulled down so that it almost covered his eyes, which were a faded blue and watery. He had a large waxed white moustache which quivered when he spoke. He was carrying a highly polished cane with a silver handle, and when she did not answer him at once, he pointed it at her with an imperious gesture.

"I'm a busy man. Don't waste my time," he said with irritation. "I repeat, why do you want to see the manager?"

"I'm looking for employment," Toria replied. "Without much success, I fear, for I'm unable to get past the doorman."

With a sweeping bow the corpulent gentleman offered her his arm. "With me you can," he said, and before she knew what was happening, Toria was inside the Alhambra and climbing the red-carpeted stairs to a room at the top with the word *Manager* printed on the door in large gold letters.

"I suppose," the man said, removing his cape and wide-brimmed hat before settling himself behind a massive desk, "I suppose you want to join the chorus. You don't strike me as the type who would relish the role of a barmaid."

He was wearing a black alpaca suit with a brilliant red vest, which made him appear even stouter. Lighting a cigar, he blew a cloud of smoke in her direction.

"I was hoping to sing," she ventured timidly.

He sighed deeply. "They all say they can sing or think they can sing," he remarked. "I suspect you have a large repertoire of romantic ballads."

"Yes, I do. I've learned some beautiful songs about—"

"Moon and June and Soon," he finished the sentence for her with a broad smile. "Well our audiences prefer comic numbers, slightly on the bawdy side, spoofing the young swells, for example, who spend their time along Rotten Row watching the girls go by. That one has been a great hit this season. No, I don't need songs about unrequited love, but I might be able to use you in the chorus—so lift your skirts and let me see your legs."

"No!" she said defiantly.

He sighed deeply again. "How," he asked with some impatience, "how can I decide if you would qualify for the chorus if I don't see your legs? They might be too fat, or too thin, or bowed or knock-kneed for all I know. I won't buy a pig in a poke."

Reluctantly, she raised her skirts, and as he kept repeating, "Higher, higher," she blushed and complied until they were well above her knees, relieved when he finally said, "All right, that's enough. Your legs are as well put together as your face, and that's saying a lot. As it happens, one of my young ladies has found it necessary, quite unexpectedly, to—er—retire. You're about her size, so you'll fit into her costumes. If you can learn the routines fast, you're hired. Ten shillings a week to start and report for rehearsal tomorrow at ten."

"Oh, thank you, sir," Toria cried out. "You see, I need a job desperately. You've saved me from—"

He raised his hand in a weary gesture. "Spare me your problems," he interrupted. "I have enough of my own. Now, what's your name?"

"Toria, I mean Victoria Leighton."

110

"A pretty name. As you've undoubtedly guessed, I'm George C. Sinclair, the manager of the Alhambra. Now don't forget. Tomorrow at ten, and the doorman will this time let you pass."

She smiled, thanked him again profusely, and was turning to leave when he gestured to her to remain.

"One word of advice before you go. I tell this to all my young ladies, though most of them give it scant attention. Stay away from the stage-door Johnnies, the canteen, and the bubbly." With a broad grin he dismissed her.

Chapter Nineteen

When Toria Leighton joined the chorus at the Alhambra, she stepped into a strange and frightening world. If it hadn't been for a grim determination never to return to a life of lowly servitude, she would not have survived the first few weeks.

She shared a dressing room with ten other members of the chorus, and although they were soon teasingly labeling her "the little Puritan," they were kind to her, showing her how to apply makeup and more than once lengthening the time of the rehearsals so she could master the steps.

From the beginning she did not find the dancing difficult, for she was lithe and supple and had been born with an unerring sense of timing. It was the Alhambra itself at night that at first almost disarmed her. The promenade with its numerous bars where women brazenly accosted the men for a drink, the coarse catcalls coming from the sixpenny gallery, the banging of pewter tankards on tabletops when some dancer on stage flung her leg higher than the others, the harsh glare of the gas lamps—all this combined to destroy her composure.

But as time went on, she adjusted to the noise and confusion, following the manager's advice to avoid the canteen. A dark, dingy room located under the stage, it was the place that most of the chorus girls repaired to between numbers, where they were treated to champagne and wine until by the end of the evening they were, more often than not, tiddly.

Also, at the conclusion of each performance, she refused the invitations of the young men who gathered outside, anxious to escort the members of the chorus to some gin mill or to Barnes in the Haymarket, a night house with an unsavory reputation.

Despite her meager salary, she always hailed a hansom to take her home, knowing full well that a girl alone after nightfall in the vicinity of Leicester Square was asking to be ravished.

She had been at the Alhambra for exactly three months when she decided to approach the manager and plead with him for a chance to sing. After all, she told herself with resolution, he won't fire me for asking. The worst thing that could happen would be for him to refuse me.

"Ah, young lady," he said when she tapped on his door and gained permission to enter. "You may not be aware of it, but I've been keeping an eye on you, and I'm glad to note that you have followed my advice to stay away from the canteen, as well as the stage-door Johnnies, which leads me to the conclusion that in addition to great beauty you possess brains."

Smiling, he motioned for her to sit down in one of the deep leather chairs beside his desk.

"It was good advice, sir," she agreed, a trifle breathless from her climb to the top of the Alhambra. "But now I have a favor to ask. Please, won't you let me sing?"

He fiddled for a while with some papers on his desk, lit a fat cigar, and finally said, "All right, sing!"

"Right now?"

"Yes, right now."

She darted a quick glance at a piano in one corner of the room. "I can't play the piano," she admitted.

"And neither can I. Simply sing me a song. I can judge without any accompaniment whether you have talent."

So she stood up and sang one of the ballads she had sung for the Prince of Wales, that long-ago evening at Sutherland House.

When she finished and summoned enough courage to gaze at him directly, it seemed to her that countless minutes ticked by as she waited anxiously for his reply.

"All right, my dear," he said at last, "we'll give it a try." He raised his hand imperiously to shut out the words of thanks that she was on the verge of pouring out to him.

"Thank me later," he advised. "And let's hope thanks will be in order and not commiserations. Surely you've been around the Alhambra long enough to realize the audience can be the very opposite of sympathetic. If they don't like you, my girl, off the stage you go."

She nodded her head. "I know, but I'm willing to take the gamble."

He teetered back in his swivel chair, blowing clouds of smoke toward the ceiling. "I'll arrange for an accompanist for you and put aside some time for practice. Let me see, do you imagine you could be ready to make an appearance in two weeks?"

"Oh, yes, without question," she replied eagerly.

He gave her a broad grin, as he had during their first meeting. "Now another word of advice from an old man," he continued solemnly. "You must appear in something absolutely startling—a gown so gorgeous, so risqué, it will make the spectators catch their breaths, and while they are recovering from the shock, with any luck they will give you a chance to sing."

Dismissed, she left his office on a high tide of happiness. On the following Sunday afternoon, she called upon her aunt, believing that she had at last established herself in a new vocation and could return to her grandfather's house, not as a helpless supplicant but as a young woman well on the road, if not to fame, at least to modest success. Besides, she was hopeful that her aunt would find it in her heart to forgive her for deciding to make the theater her career.

Chapter Twenty

As Toria approached the Leighton house, near London Bridge, it struck her as being even smaller and shabbier than she had remembered. The white wooden gate at the entrance was badly in need of paint, and as she pushed it open, it sagged with a loud squeak of protest.

The pathway was unswept and the front door scarred and spatterred with mud. Was it always like this, she wondered? Looking back, it had seemed to her at the time to be neat and spotless. Could she be seeing it now through different eyes after her sojourn in such splendid surroundings as Park Lane and Sutherland House?

She knocked on the door with trepidation and was relieved when Ann Leighton answered and not her grandfather. Her aunt's careworn face lit up with joy as without a word she gathered Toria into her arms.

"I've missed you so," Ann cried. "Come inside and I'll put on the kettle for tea. Your grandfather is away, so you have nothing to fear on that score."

Seating herself at the wooden table in the kitchen, Toria watched her aunt move slowly from stove to cupboard, as if each step were causing pain and discomfort.

"I've been ill," Ann explained, sensing that her niece had noticed the vast change in her physical condition. "I expect any day now to be told at Lucille's that they no longer have need of my services."

"And Grandfather, how is he?" Toria asked.

"A bit grumpier and more difficult to live with than ever. Often, days go by without his uttering a word. He'll eat his supper, push back his chair, and either go to the pub or to bed. As he grows older, he no longer cares about keeping up appearances. You can see the place is going to wrack and ruin."

The kettle gave a cheerful whistle, and Ann, after making the tea, joined Toria at the kitchen table. "But what I want to hear about is you! Is life with the Esterbrooks better, now that you have become Lady Clara's personal maid?"

Toria did not reply at once, torn between prevarication and a complete confession, but honesty soon won out as she discovered it was impossible to be anything but forthright with the only person in the world who had ever loved her.

Ann sat across from her, frozen with shock, her tea untouched as Toria poured out her story from beginning to end, not omitting one sordid detail. When she was finished, there was complete silence in the kitchen except for the loud ticking of the clock on the mantel. Toria bowed her head as she waited for her aunt's judgment, staring with intensity at the old, familiar cracks in the wooden table, half expecting to be told she was no longer welcome in this house. The tension becoming unbearable, she finally looked up to find nothing but love, tenderness, and great pity in Ann's face.

"You were right to leave the Esterbrooks'," her

117

aunt said with a proud toss of her head. "I admire your courage, Toria. But I fear for your safety at the Alhambra—music halls are such notoriously loathsome places, and even if your conduct is above reproach you'll still be tarred by its reputation."

"Ann, as long as I know what I am, does it really matter?" Toria asked. "Don't you see? At last I have a chance—a chance to get out of that dreadful chorus and make a name for myself. I'll earn as much as five or six pounds a week. And who knows what other opportunities might not come along. Will you help me?"

Ann spread out her hands in a helpless gesture. "What could I possibly do to help?"

"Make me a gown, a beautiful gown. I'll purchase the material. Already I can visualize it clearly in my mind. It will be of crimson velvet, tightly fitted at the waist, with a wide flowing skirt and train. It must be very low-cut. I want the audience to gasp and stare, to give me time to sing before they start banging on the tables or talking among themselves, ignoring what is taking place on the stage.

"I'll try, my dear. I'll surely try," Ann promised. For the first time since Toria's arrival there was some color in her cheeks, and her eyes were no longer dull and lifeless as she searched for paper and pen and began to make a sketch. "I'll work on it every evening after your grandfather retires. How long do I have—two weeks?"

"Not quite," Toria said. "Ten days at the most."

"No matter." Ann dropped the pen and, leaning across the table, gave her niece a hug. "It will be ready by then, I promise."

It was time to go, and as Toria opened the door

and stepped outside, she turned to Ann Leighton and said with grave solemnity, "Soon, Ann, I will be in a position to help you, to pay you back for all the sacrifices you have made for me. Just you wait and see. I will buy a fine house with a lovely garden in the rear, and you will come to live with me. That has become my greatest goal in life, and it will happen sooner than you think."

Chapter Twenty-One

An astute theatrical manager, George C. Sinclair deliberately scheduled Victoria Leighton's debut to follow an overly long act by a mediocre comedian. Having her appear late in the evening, he was gambling that the audience would be in a mellow mood, more receptive to a romantic ballad after a slapstick performance that was about to be canceled because of a disappointing run.

Her entrance was pure drama. The stage was plunged in darkness except for one small circle of light in the center, and as the curtain rose she was revealed standing in the lighted circle, her hands spread out as if in supplication, her head thrown back appealingly to the spectators in the sixpenny gallery, who responded by suddenly becoming unusually quiet and attentive.

Her crimson velvet gown had been artfully designed by Ann to expose her smooth white shoulders, to cling to her slender figure and enhance the glow of her luxuriant golden hair, which was piled high on her head, making her appear as regal as a duchess. She wore no jewelry. It would have been superfluous, detracting from the perfection of her face.

Her opening ballad spoke of unrequited love, and

because of the tragic ending to her recent romance with Viscount Covington, her bell-like voice had acquired a deeper, more mature quality. Instantly every member of the audience, who along the way had had their full share of disappointments and heartbreaks, felt that she somehow understood and was commiserating with them. Undoubtedly, the uniqueness of her talent was this ability to convince each listener that she was singing to him and to him alone. "I know you, I sympathize with you," she seemed to be saying; she never lost that rare capacity to communicate.

From the first night, she was a great success. The audience could not have enough of her, and as her popularity mushroomed, it soon led to changes in her life-style which she found extremely rewarding.

In the chorus her pay had been six shillings a week, barely enough on which to exist. Soon she was receiving five pounds a week and a dressing room of her own, which every night overflowed with flowers and cards from her many admirers—young gentlemen begging her to allow them to escort her to dinner after the performance.

She never acknowledged these notes, and this very aloofness served to further intrigue her audience. Why did she remain so distant, so remote? people wondered. As speculation about who and what she was multiplied, the mystery around her increased in its intensity.

She was only seen on the stage and leaving the theater after the performance, wrapped in a crimson velvet cape, a hood trimmed in ermine covering her golden curls as with a smile and a proud lift of her head she would climb into her carriage and depart.

She was careful with her money, although she moved to rooms in Pimlico, a more respectable neighborhood. Her only extravagances were her carriage and expenditures for her clothes, which she knew must be opulent and glamorous. Concentrating single-mindedly on her career, she put every shilling she could save in the bank for the house which she intended to buy someday for herself and Ann.

Within six months her salary rose to ten pounds a week, the highest the Alhambra paid to any of their performers. She was seriously contemplating an offer to star in a musical at the Gaiety.

Despite her success, she remained lonely, and although the scars left by Piers's cavalier and brutal treatment of her began to heal, they never vanished completely. She was normally anything but a vindictive person and probably would have eventually forgotten her pledge to humiliate Viscount Covington, if he hadn't of his own volition attempted to come back into her life.

Out of curiosity she always read the cards that were delivered to her dressing room, and when she began receiving bouquets and messages from Piers, her first reaction was astonishment that he could entertain the thought that she would have anything but hatred in her heart for him. Finding the conceit of the aristocracy beyond belief as she tore his notes into tiny pieces and tossed them away with his flowers, she began to wonder how she could strike back at him, wound him as he had wounded her.

Revenge began to haunt her, to become uppermost in her thoughts. She seized upon the notion that the best way to pay him back would be to make him play the part of a fool, believing that if she could damage

122

his inflated ego, it would enable her to cast him out of her mind forever.

Eventually, like pieces in a puzzle that in the end fit together, a plot evolved which she proceeded to carry out without hesitation. Each evening when she arrived at the theater, there was an old crone standing by the curb pleading for a coin or two. She was a toothless, hideous creature, who was surprised one night when Toria, instead of brushing past her, stopped and inquired if she would care to earn some money.

"Of course, milady," the old crone croaked, stretching out a grimy, clawlike hand.

"I mean earn it," Toria said, and when the old woman agreed with rather a doubtful duck of her head, Toria instructed her to be there the following night, and at the conclusion of the performance to join her in her carriage.

As Toria swept out of the theater after the show, people on the sidewalk were stunned to see this withered old woman from the slums of London drive off with her.

"We are meeting an acquaintance of mine near the Serpentine," Toria told the deplorable creature, covering her face with a handkerchief to ward off the overpowering fumes of gin that permeated the carriage. Handing the woman a black velvet cloak with a hood, she gave her instructions.

"What you are to do is very simple. First put this cloak on and cover yourself completely with it. When we reach Hyde Park, I will point out the bench where you are to sit, and when a young gentleman approaches you, you are to throw your arms about him and smother him with kisses. For that you will earn two crowns and the cloak." Toria pressed the coins into her grimy hand.

Telling the driver to wait outside the park, Toria stood in the shadows to watch the performance. That day she had had a note delivered to the viscount, dripping with sentimentality, telling him she too awaited eagerly the renewal of their friendship and would meet him by the Serpentine where they had once spent such a rapturous afternoon together.

The ruse went off without a hitch, and as Piers frantically struggled to disentangle himself from the clutches of the old crone, Toria thought triumphantly: now at last I have had my revenge.

But on the way back to her apartment, alone in her carriage as it sped along the streets of London, Toria discovered to her dismay that she had really obtained small satisfaction from the skillfully executed plan. Although she was no longer a servant girl under the thumb of a ruthless housekeeper and an arrogant mistress, and although she had attained success and no longer worried about how she could earn her next shilling, nevertheless her life still remained barren and empty.

She sang songs of love supremely well, but there was no love in her heart for anyone but Ann. As the tears rolled slowly down her face, she conceded that in the end Piers was the victor, for despite the fact that she no longer loved him, he had destroyed her capacity to trust or care deeply for any other man.

Chapter Twenty-Two

Victoria Leighton performed at the Alhambra for almost a year before moving to the Gaiety to rehearse in a musical that was scheduled to open in October. This fresh challenge required so much dedication and concentration on her part that she barely noticed the end of summer and the approach of fall.

She was expected not only to sing and dance but to act as well, so that until the musical was successfully launched and proved to be a hit, she had little time to brood over the loneliness of her existence. After each rehearsal, she was content to return to her rooms in Pimlico, prepare a simple supper, and tumble into bed.

Whenever possible, she visited Ann and was able to inform her aunt that her bank account was growing to the point where soon she would be able to purchase a modest dwelling. She was disturbed by her aunt's increasing fraility, and her drive to succeed gained momentum as her anxiety to be able to offer Ann a life of ease and luxury took precedence over everything else—her own aspirations becoming secondary.

The flowers and the notes continued to fill her dressing room each night. Amused to see that Viscount Covington no longer sought her company, she became intrigued, however, by another constant admirer who sent her one long-stemmed red rose before each performance. There was never a message on the coroneted white card enclosed—only his name, Alexander, the Duke of Blakesley.

She hadn't the slightest notion whether he was young, middle-aged, or old, married or a bachelor, handsome or ugly. Each evening when she opened the shiny white box, she expected to find a message requesting a meeting, only to become increasingly mystified when this did not occur.

It was December, a week before Christmas, and a light snow powdered the city. Her performance for the evening was concluded, and as she sat at her dressing table removing her makeup, the prospect of the approaching holidays, stretching ahead of her empty of any merriment or frivolity, had cast her into a mood of depression.

More than once lately, she had been tempted to accept one of the many invitations she received, but the memory of her bitter experience with Piers always won out in the end, persuading her that the risks were far too great for a few hours of pleasure.

When there was a light tap on the door, she called out "Come in," thinking it would be some member of the cast, desirous of having a chat with her before she left.

Instead, in her mirror she saw the reflection of a man whom she knew only by the name of Alex, who had rescued her one night at the Alhambra and had been prepared to defend her a second time in the garden of Sutherland House.

Tall and lean, carrying himself with an air of great

distinction, he was dressed in evening clothes, a cape folded over his arm.

Astonished, she swung about in her chair. "Who let you in?" she demanded.

"Courtesy of the management," he replied.

"He had no right—I've told him often enough I never receive stage-door Johnnies."

"I can hardly be classified as that," he replied easily, as, to her dismay, he crossed to a chaise longue and settled himself comfortably in it.

"I see," he observed, "that you've put my rosebud in water and placed it on your dressing table. I'm honored and my curiosity satisfied, for I've often wondered what happened to it."

"So you are the Duke of Blakesley," she said.

"None other, but my friends call me Alex."

She studied him with interest and a certain amount of curiosity, conceding that his method of approach was innovative and successful too, for up until now no one had entered her dressing room except members of the cast and her personal maid. He was indeed an attractive and aristocratic man. His hair, crisp and curly, was a warm chestnut color, and his dark brown eyes that were observing her gravely were remarkably large and eloquent.

"You're more beautiful off stage than on," he remarked. "Tell me, I'm curious to learn why someone so lovely refuses all invitations."

"If it is your intention to ask me to dine with you," she said icily, "I fear you are wasting your time—and mine." Turning back to her dressing table, she picked up a comb.

"How intuitive you are, Miss Leighton, guessing

that an invitation to join me for supper was on the very tip of my tongue."

Their eyes met in the mirror, and he flashed her an amused smile.

"If you were intuitive," she answered him archly, "you would have guessed that it is on the tip of my tongue to refuse."

"What a dull life you must lead, Miss Leighton," he continued. "I've been told by many that you scorn the company of all men. Won't you tell me why? Is it because you believe your aloofness makes you more provocative, or were you, perhaps, born with a loathing for the opposite sex?"

He was still smiling at her, but she did not return his smile. "Wrong on both counts," she finally said. "I don't loathe the opposite sex, although it's true I trust none of them. Let me tell you what would happen if I accepted your invitation."

Standing up and pulling her white satin robe more closely about her, she faced him squarely, her huge violet eyes filled with anger. "First you would drive me in your carriage to the Cafe Royal or possibly to Rule's, where a private room would already be reserved for us. We would be served a superb supper with a plentitude of the best champagne and wine. Beside our table there would be placed a narrow settee and in a far corner of the room a screen where I would be expected to retire and disrobe while you discreetly lowered the lights and locked the door. Now tell me honestly, isn't that precisely what you had in mind?"

"I trust, Miss Leighton, that the vivid picture you have painted was not drawn from firsthand experience?" She saw he was laughing at her, causing her fury to mount instead of subsiding.

"Everyone in London knows without having been there what occurs at the Cafe Royal and Rule's, and they are also aware that dukes and barons and other titled gentlemen do not escort women of their own class to such places, but rather actresses and ladies of the chorus. I have never desired to join the group."

He stood up slowly and gave a sigh of mock despair. "I don't suppose you'd believe me if I told you I had neither of those places in mind, delightful as I'm sure they must be. I was thinking instead of the Carlton, in the lounge, which will be crowded with respectable people—a place where no gentleman, no matter how ardently he desired it, would contemplate an improper act. On that basis, will you reconsider?"

Toria's face displayed indecision as the pendulum swung back and forth between acceptance and rejection. After all, on the two occasions they had met, he had proved himself to be a gentleman. She was on the verge of answering yes when the memory of Piers in the rose garden, pledging his eternal love and support, flashed before her eyes.

"I regret," she told him stiffly, "that this is one endeavor in which you cannot claim success. Go back to your own class, Duke, and I will remain in mine. Surely there are many charming ladies among your acquaintances who would breathlessly grasp at the chance to spend the evening with you."

"There is nothing further I can do to persuade you?" he asked.

"Nothing—not even a dozen red roses every night with a diamond bracelet among the ferns."

He rose leisurely from the chaise longue, an enigmatic smile playing on his lips. "Nevertheless, Miss Leighton," he said, "although I am not a gambling man, I would be willing to wager a considerable sum that we will soon dine together."

"Only if you succeed in kidnapping me, sir," she replied.

He dipped his head gracefully at last, accepting her decision. She heard the door close behind him. With a shrug of her shoulders, she continued to brush her golden hair before selecting the gown she would wear for the trip to her empty apartment in Pimlico—torn between satisfaction that she had successfully repulsed his advances and the onrush of sheer loneliness which engulfed her at the prospect of yet another evening spent in solitude.

As she studied her face in the mirror, she reluctantly admitted that he was extremely attractive, one of the most attractive men she had ever encountered, and that it would have been intriguing to be riding beside him at this very moment in his carriage on the way to the Carlton.

Chapter Twenty-Three

Several nights later the cast was buzzing with excitement as the word was passed from one to the other that the Prince and Princess of Wales would be in the audience.

Toria made no comment, thinking that as she had performed before the Prince once satisfactorily, why not twice? She became agitated, however, when in the interval between the second and third acts, she received a summons to appear in the royal box at the conclusion of her performance.

As she entered the private room set aside for royalty, she found herself in the midst of a dazzling scene. The room was lavishly decorated in white and gold, with a thick crimson carpet on the floor. Champagne corks were popping and waiters were passing trays of sandwiches, while the Prince and Princess of Wales stood laughing and chatting with their guests.

An equerry met her at the entrance and guided her toward them. She curtseyed gracefully before them and, as she glanced up, saw that the Princess was smiling at her in a warm and friendly manner. She was very beautiful, dignified, and stately, yet with a disarming manner that put one instantly at ease.

"Your performance tonight was outstanding," Princess Alexandra remarked.

"Thank you very much, Your Highness," Toria replied, curtseying again.

She was surprised and slightly overwhelmed when the Prince of Wales stretched out his hand to her and drew her aside. "I've been told by a friend of mine," he began, giving her a broad smile, "that you refuse to accept all invitations. Now, tell me, isn't that rather foolish for a young lady as talented and charming as you?"

"I consider it best, sir," she replied.

"He tells me that you are not a very trusting person, and with good reason, I expect."

She flushed and replied a trifle unsteadily, "Yes, sir, with good reason."

"What a pity, but would you trust me, my dear, if I were to assure you that my good friend the Duke of Blakesley, should not be placed in such a category, for in all things I have found him to be an honorable man, above reproach."

She smiled. "If you say so, sir, how could I dispute you?"

He nodded his head gravely, apparently satisfied by her response, before moving on to greet other guests.

She was not surprised when a few moments later the Duke of Blakesley approached her. "Did you enjoy your conversation with the Prince?" he asked.

"Very much."

"Did he inform you of the many sterling facets of my character?" he asked, his eyes filled with mirth.

"That he did. He informed me too that I had seriously misjudged you."

"Well then, the hour is growing late, and if you are one half as famished as I, perhaps you will join me at the Carlton for supper. Our table is already reserved. It's been waiting for us every night since first we met."

She hesitated only briefly before dipping her head and accepting his invitation. Knowing that the Prince of Wales was a notorious philanderer, she had not been impressed by his high praise of the Duke of Blakesley's character, but the yearning for some frivolity tonight won out over caution. She decided that this was her evening to gamble.

In the darkness of the duke's carriage, she could barely discern the dim outline of his face, but she had observed him long enough in her dressing room to conclude that, although he was older than Piers and not as dashing, his manner, his entire appearance reflected unfavorably on her memory of Viscount Covington. It was as if one compared an unruly schoolboy to a polished, cosmopolitan man of the world.

"How old are you, Miss Leighton?" he asked.

"I was seventeen in May. And may I ask how old are you?"

"Touché," he responded with a laugh. She thought he possessed the most melodious, pleasing voice she had ever heard. "In comparison with you, I'm an old codger—thirty-two to be exact."

"Not so old, but persistent," she remarked drily. "It must please you greatly to know you are the first man I have gone out with since my career began."

"What a tragic waste!" he said lightly. When they drove up to the entrance of the Carlton, he sprang out quickly and assisted her to the ground with a flourish.

As they entered the lounge of the Carlton and were escorted to a corner table by the headwaiter, she suddenly felt an upsurge of excitement, like a school-girl on her first day of vacation after a dreary term. She was deeply affected by the glamour of the sur-roundings—the room tastefully decorated in cream and pink, with soft lights focused on graceful palms, while the orchestra played a lively mazurka.

"You look," he said, "like a child who is seeing a Punch-and-Judy show for the first time."

"I've never been anywhere," she told him frankly.

"Tell me about your life, Victoria," he suggested.

Usually it was a subject she avoided discussing at all costs, but to her surprise she discovered she very much wanted him to know the truth about her hum-ble beginnings.

"It's very brief and dull," she began and, as she told him about her dreary childhood in her grand-father's house and what occurred thereafter, she omitted mentioning that she had never known her father and the name of the great house where she had been briefly employed as a servant girl. She was care-ful, too, to exclude the story of her love affair with Piers, finding it too bitter an experience to mention to anyone but Ann.

The supper served them was delicious, starting with oysters, followed by filet de sole with vermicelli and crayfish tails, covered with a crisp pie crust. For dessert they enjoyed Benedictines rosés and small cups of strong Turkish coffee.

She sipped the wine, a superb Moët et Chandon champagne, with caution and wondered how he would react if he were aware that the only time she had been offered a glass of bubbly had been in the company of the Prince of Wales.

She toyed with the idea of asking him if he was married, but delayed the question, surprised that she was fervently wishing his answer would be no but at the same time fearful that would be too much to expect.

As the meal drew to a close, she waited for the inevitable suggestion that they go somewhere not so public to continue their tête-à-tête. She was astonished to find herself silently pleading with him not to do so, wanting quite desperately to stave off the ending of what had developed, as far as she was concerned, into a delightful evening.

He poured himself another glass of champagne and, clearing his throat, completely bewildered her with his next remark. "I've been delegated to inform you," he said, "that you have a protector."

"A protector?" she asked with a frown.

"Yes—I'm his intermediary, and I must confess I find it a most pleasant assignment."

"I don't believe I understand."

"It's quite simple really—a friend of mine, a very close friend, wants to offer you his protection. Quite a large sum of money is involved, as a matter of fact, along with the deed to a very desirable piece of property."

At first she was too shaken to respond, as her face flushed with anger, but at last she exclaimed. "*My lord,* if this is your method of attempting to engage me in an affair, why don't you come right out with it and say so?"

He reached across the table and covered her trembling hand with his. "I am not contemplating an affair with you," he said gently. "Pleasurable as it would be—neither is your protector."

"Protector!" She mimicked the word. "Protector, which translated into plain English, means paramour. Don't think you've fooled me for one instant, my lord, plying me with champagne, delectable food, soft lights, and music. This so-called protector, whoever he may be, wants me to become his mistress and is going about it in a very circuitous and cowardly fashion. Who is this protector, may I ask? Why doesn't he present himself directly to me?"

The Duke of Blakesley sighed deeply and concentrated on lighting his cigar. "Your protector, my dear Victoria, happens to be your father."

"My father," she gasped. "You mean that after all these years my father cares that I exist? I find that impossible to believe."

"Nevertheless, it is the truth. It is also true that he was not aware of your existence until quite recently, and now he is extremely anxious to make amends."

"To make amends with money and property?"

"Yes, and I hope, I pray you'll give it serious consideration."

Still unable to absorb the shock of his words, she lifted her shoulders in a helpless gesture. "I am confused," she told him, "utterly confused. Long ago I decided it was futile to ever imagine that my father was anything but completely indifferent to me and my well-being. Over the years I've found it less painful to erase all thoughts of him from my mind. If I have any feelings left for him at all, it is hatred for how he treated my mother."

He smiled a warm and tender smile, disarming her

again, exposing her vulnerability. "Of course you're confused, my dear. Such a revelation is bound to be a great shock. But I was at a loss how else to break the news. I don't expect an answer tonight. But promise me one thing. After I take you home, you'll think about this seriously, and on Sunday—you do have a free day on Sunday?"

She nodded her head in agreement.

"Well, on Sunday, then, you'll allow me to call upon you to explain the details and show you the property your father wishes to present to you."

She did not answer him, her thoughts still in disarray.

"On Sunday I'll call upon you, Victoria—at one o'clock." He made a motion to leave, and they left the bright lights of the Carlton for his carriage.

On the way to her rooms in Pimlico, they spoke very little. He seemed to understand instinctively that she was too disturbed to engage in any conversation, that she needed time to recover from his startling revelation.

"On Sunday, then, at one?" he asked again urgently when the carriage stopped in front of her apartment.

"Yes, on Sunday," she agreed.

He bade her a pleasant, casual good night. Inside, she tossed her ermine cape on the sofa and began to pace across the room. Who could her father be, she wondered? Certainly a man of some importance, to be the friend of a duke. She was still far from convinced, however, that this strange tale could be the truth. Could she trust the duke? That became the burning question. What if it was a clever trap that

137

would spring and catch her if she consented to the proposition offered to her tonight?

She curled up on the sofa, gazing into the cold, empty hearth, too involved in her thoughts to light a fire. The face of Alexander Blakesley, serious and dignified, came back to her, and she could not believe that he would become a part of any despicable plot against her—a plan to destroy her pride, her integrity.

Finally she went to bed, and her last thought before she fell into a restless sleep was not thankfulness that her father had at last acknowledged her existence, but rather regret that His Grace was merely an intermediary, someone who had sent her roses and breached her self-imposed isolation not because he desired to see her but because he was fulfilling the wishes of a friend.

Chapter Twenty-Four

She had dined with the Duke of Blakesley at the Carlton on a Monday night. All that week she kept glancing at her calendar, impatient for one o'clock on Sunday to arrive, wondering now and then with a rush of panic if he would keep his appointment.

In the light of day, the evening spent with him appeared so bizarre that she experienced moments of doubt regarding the authenticity of his story, believing it was inconceivable that after so many years her father would take such a sudden interest in her life.

Remembering, however, that Alexander had mentioned that only recently had her father learned of her existence, his tale gained more validity. It was possible that her mother, out of pride, out of self-respect, had not told him she was with child. If such a calamity had happened to her, Toria, she was convinced that she would never have revealed her plight, being far too proud to face possible rejection, scorn, and probable refusal to give her any assistance.

With a tender smile, she noted that the shiny white box with one red rose continued to arrive each night before her performance. On Saturday there was a message above his signature—"One o'clock, Sunday" it read, alleviating her fears that he might not materialize.

She prayed for fine weather, and her prayer was answered when Sunday dawned cold but bright, with only small patches of snow lingering on the ground. She pondered a long time over her wardrobe, finally selecting a sapphire-blue satin dress with matching coat. She carried an ermine muff. Her hat was ermine too, with a saucy brim, tied under the chin with a blue velvet bow.

As one o'clock approached, she found herself on tenterhooks, glancing in the mirror again and again to be sure her bonnet was properly adjusted, allowing a few golden curls to escape.

He arrived promptly, and a question that had tormented her all week was answered. He was as handsome as she had remembered him to be, and more importantly, he had a face of great character—no callow youth with brilliant blue eyes that led one to overlook a weak chin and lips that were inclined to pout. I don't believe he would ever hurt one willingly, she thought, and holding out her hand in greeting, she returned his warm smile with equal warmth.

"I brought the phaeton," he explained as they went out onto the street. "No coachman this time. I enjoy driving it myself."

After she had climbed up the step and settled herself, he carefully wrapped a rug about her. He looked extremely dashing in a long coat with a sealskin collar and a Russian-style fur hat. The horses were matched grays, frisky and spirited. He handled them easily, deftly as they moved at a rapid pace through the streets of London.

"I was fearful you might change your mind," he said as she snuggled down under the cozy rug.

"No, for you see I'm a very curious person. Also, strange as your story was the other night, I believed you."

"Strange but true," he assured her. "I was counting on your deciding that I could never make up such a tale. After all, what would be the purpose?"

"To gain my attention, which you have certainly succeeded in doing."

"And then what?"

She blushed and avoided his glance.

He burst out laughing. "Victoria," he said, "without question you possess a devious mind. If I wanted to capture your attention, I would use methods much simpler and more direct. What can I do to convince you that I am a straightforward, no-nonsense individual? What has happened to you to make you so suspicious of every man? Has your mother's unfortunate life been the cause of your lack of trust? Without a doubt, you are beautiful and most desirable, and no one could be in your presence without being stirred, but there are men in this universe who are honorable, my child, and who would not stoop to deceive you."

His words touched her deeply as she struggled to hold back the tears. "Then we can be friends?" she asked in a tremulous voice.

"Yes, friends. And I find it a rare privilege."

"Where are we going?"

"To St. John's Wood. You'll find the property charming, irresistible, I hope. If not, your father will be gravely disappointed."

"Will you tell me my father's name? Will I not meet him?"

He shook his head with soberness. "No, that I can't do. I can never reveal his name to you. It's part of the bargain. If by any chance you did encounter him somewhere, someday, he would never identify himself. It is enough for him to be assured that you are well taken care of."

"I've managed very successfully on my own," she replied with a defiant lift of her head.

"That you have. He considers it remarkable, but the entertainment world is chancy. In addition, he believes he has an obligation to look out for your welfare. He really is anything but an ogre, my dear, as you apparently once thought."

On the outskirts of St. John's Wood, they followed a country lane and soon turned onto a narrow dirt road protected on either side by splendid trees. Here the snow had not begun to melt, and it was a veritable fairyland with the winter sunlight turning the white lawns and heavily laden boughs of the trees into thousands of sparkling diamonds. The horses hooves made no sound in the soft snow, as a rabbit, frightened by the creak of their carriage, made a crazy zigzag path in front of them.

The property, he explained, consisted of five acres of parks and woodland. The house was red brick, Georgian in architecture, not large but well proportioned, with fireplaces in each room, and indoor plumbing. In the rear were stables, with an apartment on the second floor.

"Do you approve?" he asked after they had toured the buildings. She was touched by his obvious anxiety.

They were standing in the drawing room—it was large and airy with long windows at one end overlooking a brick terrace. "Approve!" she exclaimed. "Indeed I do approve. I love it. Oh, what fun it will be to furnish."

"Then you accept?"

"Yes, I accept. How could I refuse, when a dream I have had for a very long time is being fulfilled. My aunt will be so happy here. I can see her now in the garden, a trowel in one hand, wearing a wide-brimmed straw hat to protect her face from the sun. She loves to work with flowers but has never had the time or the place for it."

"And you will be contented here too?"

"Certainly. It will be so wonderful to be away from the city streets when I am not working. Do you suppose I'll be able to have horses—not merely for my carriage but for riding? You'll never know how much I've yearned to learn to ride."

"I'll teach you if you like. There's a profusion of bridle paths around your property."

"My property," she murmured with delight as solemnly he handed her the deed.

"Sign it," he said. "Then keep it in a safe place. Tomorrow I suggest you call on a Mr. Simmonds at Barclay's on Lombard Street. He's expecting you. There you will discover that a sizable bank account has been established for you."

"I guess you could call me an heiress," she exclaimed, finding it difficult to absorb so much good fortune at one time.

He chuckled. "Yes, you certainly could be called an heiress, and as I am well versed in financial matters, I trust you will allow me to handle your affairs."

"I would be greatly relieved if you would." She crossed to the empty hearth. "Soon there will be a roaring fire here and soft rugs on the floor, with comfortable sofas and chairs. I'll want paintings on the walls too. Do you know much about art?"

"Considerably. If you agree, we'll visit some galleries and I'll aid you in your selections. But now we must go, for it is cold and damp here without a fire. Will you have supper with me once more at the Carlton?"

As she sat across from him at the same table they had shared only a few nights before, to Toria it became the perfect ending to a perfect day. Watching him sample the wine with a nod of approval, she was unable to resist asking him a question that had been in the forefront of her mind since their first meeting.

"Are you married?" she ventured.

The Duke frowned, and at first Toria suspected he intended to ignore her question, but at last he answered her. "No—but I expect to marry quite soon, for you see, due to my position, it is imperative that I select the proper wife and establish a family. In fact, I should have done so long since."

Toria burst out laughing.

"Why do you find that amusing?" he asked, lifting his eyebrows in surprise.

"I'm laughing at such a stodgy statement. 'It is imperative that I select the proper wife!'" she mimicked.

"Young girls," he replied rather stiffly, "are inclined to be silly and romantic regarding marriage, while I am forced to consider it a most serious step. I am betrothed to Lady Caroline Stanley. I've known her since childhood, and believe me when I tell you we suit each other extremely well."

144

"Is she anything like me?" Toria asked impulsively.

"Oh, dear me, no." He tossed her an amused smile. "She is tall, very stately, trained from infancy to the manner born, and—"

"And," Toria broke in with a rush, "I imagine she would be terribly shocked if she knew you were spending the evening with me. Will you keep it a secret from her? And if you do, what if she hears about this afternoon from someone else? Won't she be extremely angry?"

"I have no intention of keeping any secrets from Caroline," the Duke said sharply. "What exists between you and me, my dear young lady, is on my part the fulfilment of a promise I made to a very dear friend. Caroline will understand perfectly and in addition will applaud me for my efforts."

His words created a barrier, and to Toria the rapport that had existed between them since their first evening together was shattered.

Angry at herself for obviously annoying him, she replied in a small voice, "Forgive me if I appeared to be prying, but I can't help thinking she is much more tolerant than I would be under the circumstances. For if I were in love with you and about to be married, I would be very possessive and resent every moment you spent in the company of another woman."

"But you're not in love with me, nor I with you," he said lightly.

She gazed at him with troubled eyes as she realized that oh, so easily, she could fall in love with him. It was the first time since her parting from Piers that she felt the faint stirrings of desire as her frozen heart began to melt.

They turned to discussing other matters, the evening speeding by far too rapidly. When they parted at her door, she held her breath, willing him to ask her if they could meet again, desolate at the possibility of being left with only a cheerful good-bye, yet far too proud to be the one to raise the question.

About to leave, as if sensing her disappointment, he said with hesitancy, "If you are free sometime on Tuesday, I could help you shop for furniture."

Smiling at him, she agreed. When he had gone and she had closed the apartment door behind him, listening to his retreating footsteps in the corridor, she felt weak, as a warm glow of happiness, of elation coursed through her body.

"I'm falling in love!" she whispered in amazement to the empty room, only to have her high spirits dashed as she recalled that he was betrothed to Lady Caroline Stanley. Every instinct warned her that she should have refused to see him again—for what future could there be with a man who was contemplating marriage, a prestigious member of the peerage, far above her on the social scale, looking down from a rarefied atmosphere that most assuredly would always be out of her reach?

Recalling his proud tone when he had informed her that his future bride perfectly fit the mold he had shaped for her, it was all too clear to Toria that he was telling her that she did not. It was all too obvious that in the end someone would be dreadfully hurt, and the chances were most likely that it would be she. Once burned by Piers's rejection, could she be foolish enough to risk being burned again?

But she found the alternative, the bleak prospect of terminating their delightful encounters, impossible to accept. Unwittingly he had opened a door, and by crossing the threshold, she found herself unable to retreat.

At least I'll see him on Tuesday, she decided, and after that, there will really be no reason to see him again. Surely just one more meeting won't be harmful.

Chapter Twenty-Five

On Tuesday afternoon they drove to the Burlington Arcade, strolling leisurely through its arched hallways, intrigued by the glass-fronted shops displaying a wide variety of wares.

She was amused when Alexander told her that the furious owner of Burlington House had in the early part of the century built the arcade to ward off careless Bond Street merchants from tossing rubbish over his garden wall.

The shops contained mainly luxury goods. Toria, exhilarated by her newfound wealth, began purchasing costly items such as Oriental rugs, expensively upholstered sofas, and tables inlaid with cloisonné and ivory, as if she had been accustomed to being surrounded with such extravagances all of her life.

As they visited store after store, they soon sensed that they were engendering an undercurrent of excitement, for the Duke of Blakesley was a well-known figure among the clerks, ranking for some time as one of their more important customers.

When asked to whom the purchases should be billed, Toria replied in her high, clear voice, "to Miss Victoria Leighton," giving the address of her new home as if she had resided there for many years. The mention of her name generated even greater agitation, so it was with a certain feeling of relief that they returned to their carriage, with the coachman trailing behind bearing a large collection of the smaller packages.

At her door she invited him in for a cup of tea, and as they stepped inside, she said apologetically, "It's rather a dreary place. I rented it furnished, and as I have considered it only a temporary residence, I haven't done very much to make it cheerful and livable."

Putting on the kettle in her small kitchen, she told him of the savings she had been accumulating toward buying a house. "I had in mind a very modest dwelling," she explained. "Such a piece of property as I now own was beyond my wildest dreams. And to spend money as I did this afternoon leads me to believe that I've taken leave of my senses."

The fire in the hearth gave a warm glow to the otherwise somber surroundings. As they settled in front of it, Toria was filled with wonder at how relaxed and at ease she felt in his presence. It was as if they had known each other forever and had long since formed a relationship which could never be disrupted.

Remembering the curiosity of the clerks in the shops they had visited, she gave a rueful laugh. "I suspect," she remarked, "there were many people today who concluded I was your mistress. It is the reason why I spoke my name so loudly and clearly when they asked who was to pay the bills."

"Do you care?" he asked.

"Not really—for as soon as the news is bruited about that I am living at St. John's Wood in such a lovely place, few will believe that I purchased it on my own. Besides, once you have been a member of the chorus at the Alhambra, your reputation is lost no matter how circumspect you happen to be. But what about you?" She turned to him with a curious glance. "Aren't you disturbed to have your name linked with mine quite so boldly? Weren't you a trifle rash to shop with me today?"

His manner immediately became distant and aloof, as it had before when she had been unable to resist asking a personal question. "Believe me when I assure you it doesn't matter. My reputation is very solid and secure," he answered her with marked indifference before guiding the conversation into another channel.

It was time for him to leave and time for her to depart for the theater. As he stood at the door, shrugging himself into his greatcoat, he said regretfully, "This will be good-bye for a while. I have business which will take me to the Continent."

She made no attempt to conceal her disappointment, her recent resolution to consider this their last meeting completely abandoned. "I shall miss you," she said sadly.

"And I—you." He hesitated for a moment before, placing his hand gently under her chin and tipping her face upward, he brushed his lips lightly across her full, sensuous mouth, saying, "You are a very charming companion."

After he had gone, she lingered for some time by the dying fire, reliving their afternoon together. She touched her lips, which he had so recently touched, wishing that his kiss had been more urgent, more demanding, rather than the kind of a kiss a man would bestow on a niece or a younger sister.

She wondered again if there was the slightest possibility that his gentleness, his attentiveness, were in some measure because he was finding her enchanting, or if their meetings were still merely a duty he had agreed to perform for her father. After all, he had kissed her and called her a charming companion, and even though the kiss had been casual and the compliment lightly given, she believed she had glimpsed in his eyes yearning and unfulfilled desire.

He was gone for over two weeks, sixteen days to be exact. She counted them. She had never been lonelier. The long-stemmed red rose delivered to her dressing room each evening became a constant reminder that her life had dramatically changed and he was the cause of it—the cause of this sudden craving for love and devotion. Like a stream that has been covered with ice all winter long until a sudden thaw makes it rampant, her stifled emotions thawed too as lassitude was replaced by naked desire.

She allowed herself to dream again, youthful dreams, and at the center of those dreams was the Duke of Blakesley, no longer cast in the role of a friend, but instead passionate, ardent, demanding.

The entire cast at the Gaiety noticed that she was giving a greater depth to her performances.

Chapter Twenty-Six

On the Sunday after the Duke of Blakesley left for the Continent, Toria ordered her coachman to drive to her grandfather's house. As they passed along the familiar streets of London, crowded with vehicles of every description, she thought how strange it was that the West End of the city and the East End never mingled.

Many poor people in the poverty-stricken slum areas were totally unaware of the existence of Grosvenor Square with its stately mansions or the Regency town houses along Park Lane. It seemed to her quite remarkable that she had succeeded in bridging the gap.

Idly she wondered where Alexander lived, and it amused her to think that she had become strongly attached to this man and yet had no notion of where he resided or how he spent the hours when not sharing them with her. She could easily have made inquiries among some of her associates at the Gaiety about him, but she hesitated to do so, reluctant to arouse their curiosity, unwilling to become the butt of inquisitive questions.

Undoubtedly he was of high rank in the British aristocracy. He had a mansion in London and an estate in the country. She became determined the next time they met to attempt to dissolve some of the mystery surrounding him by penetrating his reserve.

Instead of the bulk of their conversation revolving around her and the problems of setting up a new household, she resolved to learn more about him, so that when they were apart she would be able to visualize to some extent what he was doing during their long hours of separation.

Then the unpleasant thought struck her that the times away from her were undoubtedly spent in the company of Lady Caroline, and she felt a sharp pang of anguish coupled with resentment—resentment that due to the accident of her birth she would never be considered by him or any of the members of his class to be "to the manner born." What chance in the world did she have, she was forced to concede, to replace in his affections a woman to whom he was not only betrothed, but a woman who lived in a sphere that she could only view from a distance.

She was relieved when she finally reached her old home and could temporarily banish her uncomfortable musing as she related to Ann her stupendous news. She poured out her story before her aunt even had time to put the kettle on the stove for tea.

"My father knows who I am, Ann," she cried out, "and he has given me a lovely house and enough money in the bank so that I can spend whatever I like." Beginning with the story of the delivery of a rose to her before each performance, she related all that had happened since the night the Duke of Blakesley had entered her dressing room, carefully omitting, however, the most important part—the fact that she not only greatly admired the duke but

153

fervently hoped the relationship between them would become more and more significant.

"You are certain this man is telling you the truth, Toria?" her aunt asked when her niece finally paused to catch her breath. "He is not setting you up in luxurious surroundings in order to take advantage of you? Your very aloofness from involvement with men, the mystery that has encircled you since your success, are bound to be intriguing. Could this be his way of lowering your defenses and eventually trapping you in a situation from which it would be difficult for you to become extricated?"

"Oh, no, Ann—no." Toria spoke with vehemence. "I would stake my life on the premise that he is an honorable man. He is the opposite of Piers, completely different. It is simply my father's way of giving me protection without declaring openly that he has an illegitimate child. The duke couldn't be more candid and sincere.

"Why, he told me of his own volition that he is betrothed. He considers himself simply my friend and advisor. So now, at last, you must come with me to live. There is only one stipulation we both must abide by—to never reveal the source of my inheritance."

"Nonetheless people will consider you a kept woman," Ann said, a shadow crossing her face.

"We will state, if anyone is bold enough to ask, that my success as an actress has made it possible for me to live as I choose—that and nothing more. If they wish to think ill of me, let them. Besides, you will be my chaperone."

"It would be wonderful," Ann said with a sigh, "to be free of the deadly monotony of Lucille's. I've

154

always wanted to live in the country. Father won't miss me, that's for certain. He's rarely at home anymore, spending more and more of his time with his drinking companions."

"You can garden, Ann, something you've always wanted to do. Though it is winter, I was able to see that there are rows and rows of flower beds, carefully covered and protected from the frost. Also there's an herb garden outside the kitchen door."

She went on to list the purchases she had already made at the Burlington Arcade and to ask Ann's advice on what materials she should select for draperies. When it was time to leave in order to avoid a confrontation with her grandfather, the matter was settled between them, Ann promising to give notice immediately at Lucille's, with Toria assuring her that within a month the house at St. John's Wood would be ready for occupancy.

"You look years younger already, Ann," she said as she left. "Just think, you'll be able to sleep as late as you desire in the mornings, and during the day you can do whatever you wish. I plan to hire a cook and a maid or two, so you at last will become what you always should have been, a lady of leisure."

Ann, caught up in the whirlwind of Toria's enthusiasm, began to feel almost like a young girl again and promised to drive out with her niece the following Sunday to view the property.

From her grandfather's house, Toria instructed her coachman to drive to Hyde Park, and on the way she recalled the day, which seemed very long ago, when she had hired a hansom cab and had gone to the house on Park Lane for her interview with the Marchioness of Esterbrook. She had been frightened

155

then, fearful of what might lie ahead, but her spirits had also been high. Remembering how she had pretended she was a lady of quality with a dashing gentleman by her side, she laughed aloud. Who would have guessed then, she thought, that my childish dream would come true. Closing her eyes, she felt the presence of Alexander, Duke of Blakesley and had the strangest but most comforting feeling that wherever he was on this Sunday afternoon, he was thinking of her too.

Leaving her carriage at the entrance to the park, Toria wandered through the grounds, hoping for a glimpse of Sophie along the Serpentine, for she had never forgotten the friendship that had grown up between them and how Sophie had helped her to retain her sanity at the time of Piers's deception.

It turned out to be her lucky day when she spotted Sophie some yards ahead of her, walking side by side with Ralph. Toria was pleased to see they were still together, apparently still in love, and hurrying along the path, she soon overtook them.

"Toria!" Sophie exclaimed, her eyes widening in surprise. "I never expected to see you again. I've been reading about you in the papers. What a success you have become! Ralph and I are saving up our shillings to buy two tickets to see your performance." She flashed a shy, sweet smile in Ralph's direction.

As it was too cold to seek a park bench, the three of them continued to walk, watching the skaters on the frozen lake glide over the ice, keeping time to the music of a sprightly band.

"I have so much to tell you," Toria confessed, her eyes sparkling with pleasure at the prospect of revealing to them what she had in mind. "I would have come sooner, but I dare not go near the house on Park Lane. I might collide with one of the Esterbrooks. How fortunate for me you were here this afternoon."

As they listened with increasing interest, she revealed her plan. "I've been able to earn quite a lot of money," she explained. "Recently I purchased a home in St. John's Wood. It has a stable, which is a good thing, because I already own a coach and two horses and I want to buy additional horses for riding. There's an apartment above the stables, small but attractive. I thought, Ralph, you could take care of the stables for me. I'd pay you well. You and Sophie could live in the apartment, and Sophie, if she wished, could be in charge of my kitchen. What do you think—don't you agree it's a perfect plan?"

At first they were speechless, before recovering enough to accept, thanking Toria over and over again until she raised her hands laughingly in protest. "You mustn't thank me, for you'll be doing me a great favor. And the best part of all is that you'll be able to marry. You are fortunate, so fortunate to love one another. You can't imagine how I envy you."

It was growing late, so they started back in the direction of Hyde Park Corner, Toria informing them on the way that she would move into the house within a month and she hoped they would be able to join her by then.

"No problem, no problem at all," Ralph assured her. "You'll have to forgive us, but we're still in a daze and it will take us a bit to realize our good fortune."

As they reached the entrance to Park Lane, where

Toria's carriage awaited her, she turned to Sophie and asked, "How is Lady Clara? My only regret in leaving was that I did not have a chance to bid her good-bye."

Sophie shook her head sorrowfully. "She has married Lord Harrington. Her parents hounded her to the point where she had no other choice."

"Poor Lady Clara," Toria sighed. "I don't suppose she could possibly be happy?"

"As we rarely see her, I have no way of knowing."

"And Viscount Covington?"

"He has not changed. The less we see of him the better, as far as I am concerned. He and Lady Charlotte have a town house in Belgrave Square. He is as great a wastrel as ever, Toria, already supporting a mistress. Who she is and where she lives, I do not know. My sympathies are with Lady Charlotte, although she is a rather arrogant and self-centered individual. Nevertheless, she is to be pitied."

"And Mrs. Stackhouse?"

Sophie chuckled. "You wouldn't have expected her to change, now would you? When she discovered you had gone without a word of warning, we had some tense days in the house, with old Stackhouse reiterating that she had known all along you would come to no good. When she heard you were a chorus girl at the Alhambra, I thought she was about to explode, her face became so red."

They parted, and as Toria drove back to her apartment in Pimlico, she concluded that today had been one of the high points in her life, for she had at last been able to offer to three people she cared for a chance to come out of the shadows and bask in the sunshine.

Chapter Twenty-Seven

"It's peculiar," Toria said to Ann, "how when you are a servant, cleaning and scrubbing seems demeaning, but when it is your own place, it's fun."

She was standing on a tall ladder, a damp rag in hand, carefully washing the prisms of the crystal chandelier in the dining room. A scarf covered her head, and she was wearing a simple blue cotton dress, a leftover from the clothes she had worn while working for the Esterbrooks.

Early that morning she had collected Ann, in addition to Sophie and Ralph, and after they had toured the property with cries of delight, she had sent Sophie and Ralph to the apartment over the stables to decide what furniture they needed.

Ann, with her sleeves rolled up above her elbows, was busily scouring the dining room windows. "It's a lovely house, Toria," she remarked. "We'll be happy here."

"Soon I'll hire servants. I don't want you to continue doing heavy work."

"It's fun, as you just said, when it's your own place."

They heard the crunch of carriage wheels in the driveway and Ann, peering out the window, said,

"It's a gentleman—very distinguished in a greatcoat and a fur hat."

"It's Alex," Toria exclaimed, but before she could scramble down from her precarious perch, he had entered the room.

"Welcome home," Toria called out. As she descended the ladder, he raised his arms and, lifting her down, caught her to him. His cheek was cold against hers, and as their eyes met she saw how compassionate and intelligent his were.

"I've missed you," he whispered before setting her down and releasing her.

She wanted to respond, Oh, how I've missed you too! but caution prevailed in the presence of Ann, so she merely returned his smile.

"What many talents you have, Victoria," he spoke teasingly. "You sing and dance, you say you can cook, and you clean house too." Carefully he removed a spot of dust from the tip of her nose with his pocket handkerchief.

"I've had more than enough practice cleaning house," she admitted with a rueful laugh. Looking up at him, her heart soared again before she belatedly remembered to introduce him to her aunt.

"I've told Ann the full story, Alex," she said, suddenly becoming serious. "I felt it entirely proper that the only relative who means anything to me should be informed. You can count on her to be circumspect and not reveal the circumstances surrounding my good fortune."

He was studying Ann with frank approval. "I'll have no worries on that score. It was right to tell your aunt. By the way, Miss Leighton, do you approve of Victoria's inheritance?"

"How could I fail to?" Ann's eyes were sparkling. "It's like a dream come true."

He gave her a warm smile. "I noticed," he continued, "upon my arrival that some of the furniture has already been delivered."

"Yes, we expect to be able to move in within two weeks," Toria told him as they inspected the sofas and tables in the entrance hall still in packing cases.

Toria informed him too about Sophie and Ralph, not revealing what household they had come from—determined to avoid at all costs any discussion of her tragic relationship with Piers.

One day perhaps, she thought, she would be ready to confide in him that she had once been madly in love with Viscount Covington, but at this point she was reluctant to do so, uncertain as to what his reaction might be, afraid he might be repelled if he learned she had been on the verge of giving herself to a man with such an unsavory reputation.

Although the disillusionment she had suffered at the hands of Viscount Covington had been enormously lessened since her friendship with Alexander, she still lacked the capacity to trust any man completely. At the same time, her intuition warned her that this unexpected, exciting relationship with Alex was still in the tentative stage and nothing must be allowed to endanger it. What if revealing her romance with Piers made him wonder if she were a wanton woman who would sacrifice her virtue for a passionate love affair?

"Let's walk around the grounds," he suggested. "And later do you suppose if I laid a fire in the hearth you could rustle up some tea?"

She slipped into a long fur coat, her eyes glowing

at the knowledge that he intended to remain and share her free Sunday evening. "I think we can manage more than that," she sang out happily. "We came prepared with sandwiches and cakes."

It was a crisp, cold January afternoon, and at four o'clock evening was fast approaching, casting long shadows on the lawns, which were still streaked with patches of snow.

"I'm so glad you are back," she burst out, unable any longer to contain her joy at his return. They were walking along the driveway side by side. "Tell me," she asked, "did you have a successful journey?"

"Very." He reached out and grasped her arm as she skidded on a piece of ice. "I was in Paris, arranging for a visit of the Prince of Wales. There were a myriad of details to iron out, but it went more smoothly than I had expected."

"You know the prince that well?" she exclaimed, glancing up at him with an expression of awe.

"Yes, I often assist him." They had come to the edge of the woods, and he motioned to a clearing where two deer stood motionless, still unaware of their approach. A moment later the deer had vanished, and they heard the sharp crack of a branch as it tumbled to the ground.

"They are so proud and graceful," she exclaimed. "I'm just beginning to discover all the wonderful facets of country life."

"Yes, I've never been able to contemplate stalking them. On my estate, Uplands, we have many deer. They come down from the hills in search of water. Late at night and early in the morning you can see them drinking at our pond. You must visit Uplands

162

some day soon to meet my mother. You'd be bound to like her, and I know she would like you."

"Lady Caroline would not object?" she asked with a tremulous smile.

"Certainly not. I have told her about you, and she has already suggested that you and she should become acquainted."

The prospect of meeting his fiancée—of watching the two of them together sharing intimate glances— made her give a sudden shiver. "Let's go back to the house," she said quickly, "for if you are as cold as I am, you must be anxious for tea."

While he built a fire, she and Ann busied themselves in the kitchen, unpacking the hamper they had brought and heating water in the kettle.

Later, when Sophie and Ralph joined them and were introduced to the Duke of Blakesley, they gathered around the fire, spending an hour or two discussing what pieces of furniture they would place where, agreeing that for the time being what fun it was to be in an empty room, sitting cross-legged on the floor enjoying their supper.

As darkness fell and it was past time to leave, Toria's face flushed with pleasure when Alexander instructed her coachman to take the others home, asking her to share his carriage on the drive back to London.

"Tell me more about Paris," she asked eagerly when they were alone. "What did you do? What did you see?"

He laughed, captivated by her enthusiasm. "This trip was largely business," he explained, "although I did attend the opera and a musical that was highly amusing. I thought of you constantly during both performances, of how much you would have enjoyed Wagner's exquisite love music and how much more skillfully you would have handled the leading lady's role in the play."

"Paris, the city of love," she murmured. "Isn't that what it is called, Alex? Doesn't the Prince of Wales consider it the most romantic place in the world?"

They had reached the outskirts of London, and in the soft glow from the streetlamps she was able to discern his face—the finely chiseled nose, the dark, liquid brown eyes, the lips curled in a half-smile which was strangely sad.

"Yes, without question it's the city of romance. Do you suppose that is why, while there, my thoughts turned frequently to you?"

"Did they, Alex? I'm glad, for my thoughts were constantly with you."

"Incidentally, I bought you a gift. When I saw it, I said to myself, this is for Victoria. It should hang over her mantel at St. John's Wood."

"A painting! How lovely! When may I see it?"

"It will be delivered soon, and when we place it on the wall, we will open a bottle of champagne in celebration."

"Alex," she said gently, "I missed you so dreadfully I counted the days—sixteen of them plus eight hours, from the moment you left me until you returned. I can't seem to erase you from my mind, Alex. What am I going to do?" As she spoke she felt a gnawing fear possess her that she had been foolish to betray her despair, her uncertainties, afraid he might decide it was time to sever their relationship.

He turned to her, his dark eyes full of love and

devotion. Without a word he drew her to him, and when their lips met, she was swept to the very pinnacle of bliss. This time it was a lover's kiss, clearly revealing the extent of his passion.

When he finally released her, she gave a shuddering sigh and rested her head on his shoulder, while his fingers tenderly stroked her thick golden hair. "What am I going to do?" she repeated, a note of desperation creeping into her voice. "It would be foolish of me to deny that I love you." She raised her head and, searching his face, saw that it was white and strained.

"On the evening we first met, Victoria, I swear I never entertained for one second the notion that it would come to this, that every hour apart from you would become meaningless. I'm in love with you too, my darling, hopelessly in love for the first time in my life."

"Well then, Alex," she cried out, deliriously happy that he had declared himself, "there is no problem. How fortunate we are to have discovered our true feelings before you married Lady Caroline. How tragic it would have been if, before we met, she had become your wife."

His body stiffened, and the hand that had been tenderly stroking her hair was withdrawn. "But, Victoria," he said, "I am not free. Don't you understand that any future for us is out of the question?"

"No, I don't understand." Her eyes flashed with anger. "Is it because of your rank, your position? Or is it because you are in love with Caroline, while I am only a passing fancy?"

The minutes dragged by before he answered, and when he did it was obvious that every word he uttered caused him pain. "I care too much for you not to be honest. Surely you are far too intelligent to believe it is possible for me to marry outside my class. When I became the Duke of Blakesley, I shouldered heavy responsibilities which I can never place in jeopardy. I owe allegiance not only to my father's memory, but also to the other members of my family and the people on my estates who depend upon me. Caroline has lived her entire life in the same environment. That is why our betrothal is exactly right and cannot be altered. Besides, I have asked for her hand and she has accepted. I could never break my promise. Would you admire me if I did?"

"To put it bluntly, what you are saying is that I am beneath you." She flung the words at him with unconcealed contempt.

"Certainly not beneath me, except by accident of birth. You possess all the qualities a man could ever want in a woman—beauty, intelligence, and spirit. Please, Victoria, forgive me if what I have said has hurt you, but remember, you asked me to be frank." His voice was gentle, replete with sorrow.

The carriage had stopped in front of her apartment. The horses moved restlessly in the cold, and the coachman, who had climbed down from his box, was stamping his feet on the icy pavement.

"I could never contemplate an affair with you," he added, making no move to leave the carriage. "I love and admire you too much for that."

"To think," she said, attempting a weak smile, "that on our first evening together I was convinced it was what you had in mind."

He was smiling now too. "I'll never forget that night. It will be engraved on my mind forever. How utterly adorable you were when you believed you were defending your virtue. Although I must admit, my darling, it is becoming increasingly difficult for me not to sweep you into my arms and carry you off to Paris."

"Without benefit of clergy?" she asked sardonically, her hand resting on the carriage door, her head erect and proud, her eyes flashing. "That is something, my dear Alex, you will never accomplish. If I am not good enough for you to marry, and you've made your position on that score extremely clear, I see only one solution to our predicament—we must say good-bye."

She slipped out of the carriage, not allowing him an opportunity to offer any assistance. Before she slammed the door behind her, she threw him a challenging glance. "To think, Alex, you'll never know what you have missed!"

The corridor leading to her rooms was empty, with only one weak lamp lighting the way. It was dark and chilly inside. She shivered as she drew her cloak more closely around her and lit a fire in the hearth.

At least he was honorable, she conceded. Not like Piers, who would willingly have told any lie to capture her affection. Also, despite the hurt it caused her, she knew he was simply following the code he had inherited at birth when he had declared he could never marry a woman who had once been a servant girl and later in the chorus at the Alhambra, and who had been born illegitimate.

She drew nearer to the flickering fire, stretching out her hands to gain some warmth, regretting that she had consented to dine with him on that night

167

long ago at the Carlton House, that she had laughed with him, talked with him, and allowed him to storm her defenses.

The days and nights ahead without him stretched before her endlessly. She felt as if she had entered a dark tunnel from which there was no escape, for if they could not marry and were unwilling to engage in a love affair, she could envision no future as all doors closed firmly and irreversibly behind them. To her there was only one recourse—to forget him as she had forgotten Piers.

She began to work longer hours at the theater, arriving early for extra rehearsals, hoping that if she gave more of herself to each performance, it would lessen the impact of her loss. In February she moved to St. John's Wood, discovering that without Alex she no longer had any desire to set up her own establishment.

The weeks dragged by slowly, monotonously. It was not until a gloomy Sunday afternoon in March, with a cold rain dripping from the eaves, obscuring the gardens, that Alex returned. She had been prowling restlessly about the house when she heard a carriage coming down the road. Hurrying to the front door, she opened it to see him stepping onto the gravel driveway, struggling with a large package.

"I have the painting I bought you in Paris," he called out. "I felt it was only right to deliver it to you in person."

He hesitated on the stone steps. It was the first time she had ever seen him unsure of himself, so she dispelled the awkward moment by asking him to come inside. "I wouldn't want to be responsible for causing you to catch a chill," she said.

He placed the package carefully on the hall table, removing his gray topcoat and homburg, which were soaked by the rain, as with a grin he rescued a bottle of champagne from his pocket. "Remember, I promised you we would celebrate?"

"I thought we had agreed to say good-bye," she said stiffly, refusing to take the bottle from his outstretched hands or to look at him directly.

"It was you who said that, Victoria, not I. At the time I considered it best to go along with your decision, to attempt to forget you, but all attempts have proven to be a dismal failure. If we cannot marry or be lovers, can't we at least be friends? I promise I won't make love to you again, but couldn't we ride together, sit in front of the fire and talk, and meet for dinner now and then? Please, Victoria, I beg of you. Let me share a portion of your life."

She found herself unable to refuse him. "You win, Alex," she whispered. "I can't forget you either."

Swiftly he moved toward her, as with a tender smile she raised her hands in a gesture of protest. "Friends, Alex, nothing more," she reminded him. "Now may I see my painting?"

She watched him as he unwrapped it carefully. "It's a Renoir," he explained.

Toria was speechless for a moment, captivated by its sheer loveliness. Although not a connoisseur of art, she recognized immediately that it had been created by a master. It was a pastoral scene, the colors luminous, glowing, iridescent. Against the white walls in the drawing room, it glowed like a precious jewel.

"Alex, I'll treasure it always," she exclaimed.

He uncorked the champagne and filled two fluted glasses.

"To Renoir!" Victoria said.

"To us!" Alexander replied. He crossed to the window and drew back the curtains. "The rain has ceased, the sun is shining. It's a good omen, Victoria, when the world smiles upon our reunion."

Chapter Twenty-Eight

Spring came early that year, giving Toria and Ann their first opportunity to see the countryside awaken from its long winter of slumber. Each day brought a fresh revelation, and to Toria it dovetailed perfectly with her growing love for Alexander. The budding trees, the lawns turning from brown to green, the songs of sleepy birds at dawn all were clarion signals to her that the world was no longer a dismal place, but bursting with joy and wonder.

Sometimes she even became half convinced that Alex was wrong when he said he could never be free, and that as his love for her increased, the obstacles keeping them apart would miraculously disappear.

By May, Ann was spending long hours in the gardens. Two men were hired to assist her, as there was too much for one individual to handle, but the herb garden off the kitchen wing became hers alone.

Sophie proved to be an excellent cook, and with a girl hired to work in the kitchen and two others in charge of household tasks, the staff not only balanced each other very well but were content, because the pay was liberal and both Miss Leightons proved to be fair and compassionate.

With Alex's advice Toria had purchased two

horses at Tattersall's—a gentle gray mare named Ruby for herself and a spirited chestnut for him to ride. Ralph, sole proprietor of the stables, never failed to see that the horses were curried and well fed.

Since the decision to continue their relationship on a strictly platonic basis, Toria and Alex had managed to honor this pledge. The ardent kisses exchanged that evening on the ride to Pimlico were not repeated, although during their frequent meetings, their eyes would often meet, expressing deep regret that the love they held for each other could never be theirs to savor.

Whenever possible, Alex dined with her after a performance, and she began to discern what an important man he was—a prominent figure in the House of Lords and a confidant of the Prince of Wales, as well as other members of the royal family.

His trips out of the country and to distant parts of the British Isles meant long and difficult separations, but unless he was on some journey, Sunday belonged to them alone. On that day he would arrive early at St. John's Wood and linger until long after nightfall.

Often, as they rode together down a country lane that led to the bridle paths through the woods, they would pass a smart victoria with a middle-aged woman seated behind the driver. She would wave and smile at them pleasantly and they would return her greeting. She was always alone, tightly laced into an opulent silk or satin gown, with a florid face and a liberal sprinkling of jewels on her plump fingers.

"I wonder who she could be," Toria asked curiously after several such encounters.

Alex hesitated a little before replying. "Her name is Tillie Jones, a very well known comedian. She was the sweetheart of the Alhambra many years back. Probably you are too young to remember her."

"What does she do now?"

He pointed his riding crop toward a large white house in the distance. "She lives there, your neighbor, but I wouldn't encourage her friendship, Victoria."

"Whyever not?" She gave him an inquisitive glance. "Surely you of all people are not adverse to actresses."

"It's not that."

She saw he was about to become evasive, so pressed her point. "Sometimes it's lonesome here. Why shouldn't I be neighborly?"

They rode along without speaking for a while, until Alex broke the silence by saying, "I'd never want what has happened to Tillie to happen to you, my darling Victoria. I've seen too much of it. When a woman becomes a man's mistress, it can easily deteriorate into a coarsening experience, and it is inevitably the woman who ends up the loser. I know it should not be, that's it's totally unfair, but no matter how deeply they love each other at the outset, either the man eventually tires of it or the lady in question grows restless with the scraps from his table. She becomes discontent, no longer satisfied with her position, and turns to pursuits that are degrading, distasteful. Do you see now why I am so adamant that we should never become involved in an affair?"

It was cool and quiet in the woods. When they reached a narrow bridge that crossed a stream, they tethered their horses and leaned against the wooden railing, watching the waters of the brook, swollen from spring rains, racing with a steady roar to the river and thence to the sea.

"I want you to meet my mother," Alex spoke quietly, his eyes fastened on the turbulent stream. "Remember once I told you she spends most of her time at Uplands? Next weekend she is entertaining a few friends and has asked that you join them."

Startled, Toria stared at him in surprise. "You mean your mother is not averse to having me as a guest?" she exclaimed.

"Yes, I've spoken to her of our friendship. Why should that disturb her? She knows I am extremely fond of you and is quite anxious to make your acquaintance."

"But, Alex, as you are betrothed, isn't it difficult for her to accept your friendship with another woman, even if she's assured it is a platonic one?"

Her hand was resting on the railing close to his, and as their fingers touched, she discovered that even such a casual gesture caused her to tremble.

"Besides," she continued, "I doubt if I would have the courage to meet Caroline. I said once I would be able to do so, but now I'm not sure. It would be very painful for me in her presence to act as if you and I were casual friends—nothing more."

"Caroline will be there, although she is in Paris now—replenishing her wardrobe."

"For her trousseau?" Toria asked hesitantly.

"Yes, the wedding will be soon."

"Next month?"

"Yes, next month."

"Don't tell me the day," she declared swiftly. "That would be too much for me to bear."

"I should have informed you before this that our

174

marriage was soon to take place. It was cowardly of me not to do so." His voice had become low and husky, and as she watched him concentrating on the tumbling waters, he had never appeared more handsome to her than he did at that moment in his tweed riding jacket, his white shirt open at the throat, his chestnut colored hair tossed by the wind.

"Alex," she said with a great effort, "since I can't be your wife or your mistress, I am discovering that it is becoming more and more impossible to be near you. Sooner or later we must say good-bye. It isn't fair to Caroline for me to continue encroaching on your life. Someday in her presence we will reveal our deep love for each other, and she will learn the truth. How can we constantly keep our emotions buried? I find each time we meet more difficult."

At last he turned his attention from the stream to her. "You mean," he asked, "that you want us to separate permanently? We tried it once—unsuccessfully."

"We'll simply have to be successful this time. Not so long ago, I carved out a new life for myself. I'll try again. I may take a trip to Europe with Ann. New surroundings might make it less difficult to forget."

When he did not answer, she added, "I see no other solution, do you? Haven't you felt all along that eventually it would come to this?"

Slowly he nodded his head in agreement. "Yes, it was inevitable. But each time I have reached the point of parting, I have shied away from such a final decision, saying to myself—just one more time. But you're right, of course. Once I am married, the situation will become very difficult. But I do have one last request, Victoria. Will you come to Uplands this weekend if I promise you it will be our farewell and that after it is over, I will never bother you again?"

"Do you think it would be wise? Won't it serve to make our parting even more onerous?"

"Probably, but I find I am tiring of always doing the wise, the proper thing. Besides, I have a deep desire to show you Uplands, the places there that mean so much to me. I want you to remember me, and I want to remember you in that setting. I have this craving to be with you there, to share with me, if only briefly, its timelessness, its beauty. Then I can always think back and say, Victoria was with me here. We strolled together in the gardens, we sat before the fire in the study and rode through the woods in the early morning before the rest of the world had awakened. Perhaps too it will help you to understand why I view my inheritance, my responsibilities, with such gravity."

Nervously, she agreed to make the journey to Uplands, and as they mounted their horses and rode through the still woods, she had the sudden thought that maybe if he saw her in such a setting, he would cast aside his carefully constructed arguments against marrying her and at last plead with her to become his wife.

That night after he had departed, she repeated to her aunt the conversation she and Alex had had during their morning ride.

"We love each other so much, Ann. It seems so unfair, so terribly unfair, that he clings to outmoded precepts and ideas, making him unable to see that he is foolish to marry someone he does not love, no

176

matter how well she fits the mold he has fashioned for his wife."

"Darling," Ann said gently, her heart aching for the torment Victoria was experiencing, and feeling completely helpless to alleviate the pain. "Haven't you learned yet the lesson that life is more often unfair than not?"

"It is a lesson I can't accept," Toria burst out. "I truly believe that if it weren't for the memory of what happened to my mother, I would not hesitate to confront Alex and demand that we live together. Surely a few months or maybe years of bliss is preferable to none at all."

"Don't be so rash," Ann exclaimed, thoroughly aroused.

"Don't worry, Ann. It will not happen, for even if I found the courage to take such a drastic step, Alex would turn me down. So I will go to Uplands. I will grant him this final request, and after that it will be my task to learn to live without him."

Feeling drained of all emotion, Toria kissed her aunt good night and went to bed, comforted to some degree by having poured her grief out to someone she could trust. Surely, she thought, it is selfish of me to expect nothing less than perfection in the road ahead. I, at least, have had many hours of joy in Alex's presence, while some people, such as Ann, have never experienced what Alex and I have shared.

As the weekend of the house party drew near, she convinced herself that she and Alex would be able to carry on as they had in the past for one more time, and when the weekend was over, she would be able to say farewell with dignity and no outward signs of regret.

But she failed to fully comprehend that a love affair with no prospect of consummation often becomes not only complicated and frustrating but as difficult to control as a skittish horse that bolts and runs away with its rider.

Chapter Twenty-Nine

Badly in need of a vacation from the theater, Toria arranged for her understudy to temporarily take over her role, busying herself with the delightful task of selecting new clothes for her sojourn at Uplands. She felt that if her appearance was right, she would adjust to unfamiliar surroundings more rapidly and with greater ease. In the end she purchased an outfit for every conceivable occasion.

It was Thursday, the day before her departure. She was surprised when one of the maids entered the library, where she was reading, to announce that she had a visitor. It was the first such announcement since their arrival at St. John's Wood, and she waited with interest to see who her caller might be.

When it turned out to be Tillie Jones, she greeted her with a mixture of pleasure and apprehension. Assuring herself that Alex would not object to such a casual visit, she rang the bell and ordered tea.

"You have a very lovely place, Miss Leighton," Tillie Jones remarked, crossing to a chair by the hearth. Arrayed in a red silk gown which only served to emphasize her corpulence, she accepted the offer of a cup of tea graciously and attacked a plate of sandwiches with unconcealed delight.

"You enjoy country living?" she asked, her bright, inquisitive eyes darting about the room, observing the richness of the Oriental carpets and that the chairs and tables were of the highest quality.

"Very much," Toria replied. "It's a welcome change from the rapid pace in the city."

"I've seen your musical twice. You're very good."

"Thank you. I understand that not so long ago you were the idol of the Alhambra."

"I was, but fame is fleeting, my dear. I was smart and feathered my nest, if you know what I mean." She studied Toria's expensive afternoon gown, a diaphanous Chinese silk creation. "It's plain to see," she added, "that you are doing the same thing. Tell me, my dear, who's paying for all this?"

Toria found it difficult to contain her anger. "I am, of course," she replied curtly.

"If you say so, my girl," her visitor replied with a malicious smile, "but being familiar with the theater, I can guess that the amount of money you're earning wouldn't be enough for you to live in the style to which you seem accustomed. Take my advice and keep the man guessing, and you'll end up with twelve horses in your stables instead of four."

"Miss Jones," Toria said wearily, "what can I say to convince you that I am not living in sin?"

"My apologies, Your Ladyship." Tillie's voice took on the mimicking tones of a professional comedian before she switched to the subject of the latest trends in fashion, coming out strongly in favor of lower necklines for more exposure of the delightful attributes she proudly possessed.

"I've never been shy about the gifts God has bestowed upon me," she finished airily. "Though I

180

must say, Miss Leighton, you're a bit on the scrawny side for much décolleté."

Toria did not respond, watching with amazement as Tillie Jones, having polished off the sandwiches, tackled a plate of fancy cakes with gusto. She was relieved when Ann came in from the garden, hopeful that by introducing her aunt she could prove she possessed some measure of respectability.

"Miss Jones is our nearest neighbor, Ann," Toria explained. "She lives in the white house on the hill. that we pass on our way into the city."

"You must attend one of my parties," Tillie Jones continued. "I have something going on over there most every weekend, and when things get dull I go out in search of fun. Last year a bunch of us went to the Goodwood races. Have you ever gone there?"

Toria and Ann shook their heads mutely. "Well, I filled up my barouche with some lady friends of mine and off we went. The Goodwood Cup is as high-toned as Ascot but a shade more informal, as there's no royal enclosure. We were dressed to the nines, we were, and took along a huge picnic basket and plenty of bubbly.

"It was great sport to watch the toffs crowd around our carriage, like bees buzzing around a pot of honey, and the more they buzzed about and the more we laughed and exchanged a joke or two, the stiffer and frostier their womenfolk became. It was great sport to watch those stiff-necked ladies attempting to keep their dignity. I'll include you in our next outing if you like."

"Thank you," Toria replied coldly, "but we seem to keep very occupied right here at our own place. I doubt very much if we could spare the time."

Tillie Jones gave her a sharp look, shrugged her massive shoulders, and lumbered laboriously to her feet. "I was just trying to be neighborly," she snapped. "I'm not one to hold a grudge, so you're welcome to return my call." With a curt nod of her head, she swept out of the house and into her waiting carriage.

"What was that all about?" Ann demanded, thoroughly confused by the abrupt departure.

Consumed with rage, Toria burst out, "That odious creature accused me outright of being Alex's mistress. Nothing I said could dissuade her. I've never been so insulted."

"But Toria," Ann protested, alarmed by her niece's unusual display of temper, "you must admit that to outsiders it appears that way. Now come, let's have a glass of sherry and discuss more pleasant things." When Toria did not answer, she added gently, "I trust you didn't insult her."

"No more than she deserved, but if so I doubt she'll remain insulted for very long. She has a hide as thick as an elephant's."

Calming down, she poured sherry from a decanter for herself and Ann, only half listening as her aunt launched into a detailed description of what she was accomplishing in the garden.

Thoroughly disturbed by her strong reaction to her visitor's remarks, Toria kept reassuring herself that what had occurred this afternoon was something she should have been prepared to accept without taking umbrage. Nevertheless, she was discovering, to her dismay, it was one thing to be aware of what people were thinking and say airily to yourself, "I don't care—It doesn't matter—It's what

182

I am that counts," and quite another matter to hear the charge directly from a stranger.

Although she tried to rid her mind of the unpleasant incident, she was unable to do so as Tillie Jones's visit continued to haunt her, overshadowing pleasant daydreams about the coming weekend.

Certainly, she told herself, the guests at Uplands would never be so cross as to speak to her as Tillie Jones had, but what if there were sly innuendos or covert glances of amusement when she and Alex appeared together?

With a great effort she forced herself to think of other things, realizing that it was fruitless to spoil the prospect of a weekend with Alex by trying to change a situation which was unchangeable. Determined to avoid discussing her tea with Tillie Jones with Alex, she at last gave herself up to the delightful thought that soon she and Alex would meet again.

Chapter Thirty

As the train pulled into the tiny station in the town of Bedford, she saw that Alex was already there, waiting for her. She spotted him immediately on the platform, terribly handsome in his casual country tweeds, eagerly searching for her among the passengers.

She had promised to arrive early, so they could spend some time together before the onslaught of the dowager duchess's other guests. From London to Bedford there had been rain, a gentle spring rain, but now as she stepped onto the platform the sun found an opening in the gray clouds, giving the trees around the station an iridescent glow. She lifted her face toward its warmth and thought—it's clearing, a good omen.

"It's going to be a lovely weekend after all," he called out, and reaching her side, he grasped her waist and, lifting her from the ground, spun her about as she laughingly protested.

"I've missed you," he said. "A week without seeing you is a lost week. You are even more beautiful than I remembered. Country life agrees with you, my darling."

"Oh, Alex," she exclaimed, "I've missed you too

—dreadfully, but," and she shook her head at him reproachfully, "this will never do. I thought we had agreed to be extremely circumspect, so that your mother's guests would assume we were merely on a nodding acquaintanceship."

"But as they haven't arrived yet and won't until four, the agreement is not in effect. So come on, we have precious hours all to ourselves, and there's so much I'm eager to show you."

He collected her luggage, and she followed him to his surrey, thankful to see that he had driven in alone.

"How far to Uplands?" she asked.

"Six kilometers, roughly," he said as he placed her baggage in the rear. Helping her into the front seat, he swung himself up beside her.

She was wearing a rose silk dress trimmed with lace, and a large picture hat with a soft white plume. Laughing down at her, he removed her hat. "In order to see your glorious hair," he explained as he snapped his whip and the surrey pulled away from the curb.

"You're acting like a schoolboy," she protested. "I've never seen you so carefree."

"You're right. I haven't been so carefree in a long time. When I awoke this morning, my first thought was—she is coming! She will be here with me very soon in my ancestral home, and the fact that the rain was streaming down the window panes didn't distress me in the least."

"It's clearing now." She pointed to the large patches of blue sky. "Are we going directly to Uplands?"

"No, I told my mother not to expect us until tea-time. First I want to show you the village, then we'll lunch at the local inn and after that explore the countryside."

"But what about Caroline?" she asked. "Won't she be disturbed when she arrives at Uplands and finds you aren't there?"

His face sobered. "Caroline comes tomorrow morning—in time for the hunt. Today is ours alone, perhaps the last one we will be able to share. Now, I beg of you, let's forget about my mother, her guests, and most of all, Caroline. Let us pretend, if only for a few hours, that there are just two people in this entire world—you and me."

She smiled at him, a warm, tremulous smile. "Which won't be difficult for me to do. Do you real-ize, Alex, how seldom we have the chance to really be alone, except on our occasional rides around St. John's Wood? I guess if even Caroline knew we were stealing a few hours, she wouldn't object too much. After all, soon she will be spending the rest of her life with you."

Leaving the surrey with a stableboy at the inn, they wandered leisurely along the main street of Bed-ford, pausing to peer into shop windows, to browse through the bookstore, to meet the local grocer, who called Alexander "Your Grace," and to join in the laughter when Alex confessed that once, when a small boy, he had filched an apple from one of bins and had been caught red-handed.

"It probably saved me from a life of crime," he concluded. "I've always been grateful to you, Mr. Baskins, for having such a sharp eye."

"What was your punishment?" Toria asked, her eyes dancing.

"Nothing. Mr. Baskins is a good sort and didn't tell my parents. But we had a man to man talk about why it was wrong to steal, which cured me once and for all of at least that flaw in my character."

"You have other flaws?"

They were out on the street again, wending their way back toward the inn, and he stopped, becoming suddenly serious. "Yes—don't we all? But I fear my worst flaw is that I desire you too much."

"We promised—" she began.

"I know. The subject won't come up again."

As they sipped sherry on a shaded terrace in the rear of the inn, Toria said, "There is so much I have yet to learn about you. I know you attended Oxford, but where else did you obtain your education?"

"Eton, and prior to that, tutors. I led the life of the typical younger son of a British aristocrat. Frequent trips abroad. A year in Germany to study the language."

"Younger son?" She looked bewildered.

"Yes, I guess I never mentioned to you that I had an older brother, Rupert. It's still a very painful recollection. He was killed in India while on duty with his regiment. He was just a lad when he died. That left me the sole heir to the dukedom."

He sat in somber silence for some time, staring moodily into his glass of wine. "My father never recovered from the shock of Rupert's death, so I shouldered a great deal of responsibility at an early age."

They were served luncheon in the dining room of the inn, a cheery, spotless place with whitewashed walls, low beamed ceilings, and a fire in the stone hearth to ward off the dampness from the morning's rain.

"Strong fare," Alex commented with a chuckle as he tackled the meat pie. "By Monday we will all have consumed far too much, beginning with a lavish tea this afternoon, followed by a sumptuous dinner—"

"Concluding with supper before retiring and a huge breakfast the next morning. Remember," Toria said with a smile, "I was a servant once, so I know the routine of a country weekend, although this time I'm thankful to be on the receiving end."

"I keep forgetting you were a servant at the Esterbrooks'. Remember that night in the garden when you stumbled into my arms? I've often wondered since then who had been annoying you. I suspected it might have been that rascal Piers, but then I imagine that is a period in your life you would prefer to forget."

"I rarely think of that time at all anymore. I'm thankful I had the wits to leave, although looking back I realize what a gamble I took. It was sheer luck that the manager of the Alhambra took pity on me. Without his help, I don't know where I would have ended."

"He undoubtedly recognized talent when he saw it. I find it not only amazing, Victoria, that you had the courage to strike out on your own, but also the wisdom to avoid the many pitfalls most girls in the chorus line stumble into."

"Mr. Sinclair was very wise. He gave me good advice. I followed it."

"That night when I came to your dressing room,

frankly using underhanded methods to gain access, you were suspicious, frightened. I wondered then as I have wondered since why you were so extremely fearful?"

"That should not be difficult to understand. I was completely alone. I had seen enough of the murky side of the theater to avoid taking risks at all costs. You, a man of the world, a cosmopolitan, must know what happens to girls who give their favors lightly. I saw the results of that at the Alhambra and decided early on that it was not for me." She smiled and continued her reminiscing. "But somehow that night was different. You'll never know how much I wanted to accept your invitation. I was lonely. I did so want to enjoy a little gaiety."

"Yet you were afraid of me?"

"Of course I was. I thought you were like all the rest. I was afraid to take the chance."

"Are you sorry now that later you did?"

"Sometimes, for I see no happy ending."

He covered her hand with his. "I've been very selfish, Victoria, to fall in love with you, to let you fall in love with me and to offer you nothing but a tenuous friendship."

"You must not blame yourself, Alex. My problems are not solely because of you but due to my personality." She spoke earnestly. "It's not your fault that there has always been something in me that made it impossible for me to be content to stay in my own class. Even as a child, I was determined to break away from my environment. I succeeded in doing it, not fully understanding the consequences. Not only can I never return to my humble beginnings, but I can never join the upper class. Perhaps as you said once, my problem is the accident of my birth. It's amusing when you look at it from that point of view. My grim determination to rise above my station in life placed me where I am accepted nowhere. I can't go back, and yet I can't go ahead. But come now, no more of such gloomy discussions. What are your plans for the afternoon?"

After luncheon they drove in the surrey into the lush green countryside, through woods that were dank and deep, to a pond hidden among the trees, which Alex considered his secret place. There was a wooden dock with a skiff tied up beside it. "I fish here often," Alex told her, "or perhaps it would be more accurate to say I drift on its surface with a rod in my hand, thinking and dreaming. Since we've met, my thoughts and dreams have been entirely of you."

He assisted her into the skiff, and as they glided over the quiet waters, the rhythmic dip of the oars and the warm sunlight on their faces combined to create a euphoric mood. For a brief time they forgot that this idyllic moment would soon be over and would never occur again.

Ahead of them a fish jumped, ruffling the smooth surface of the pond in widening circles, and a startled deer which had come down to the water's edge to drink wheeled and plunged back into the forest.

It was growing late when they reluctantly returned to the surrey. "The guests will have arrived by now," Alex remarked. "Will you be disappointed if we are late for tea?"

She smiled and shook her head. "Regret missing tea when we have been in paradise?" she asked and resisted adding the dismal fact that it was to be their last time in paradise together.

He must have been thinking the same painful thought, for his face grew somber, and they drove the rest of the way to Uplands in silence.

Chapter Thirty-One

When Toria caught her first view of Uplands, she found it even larger and more impressive than Sutherland House. Following a dirt road through the woodlands and meadows sweet with clover, they finally reached a stretch of well-clipped lawn and formal gardens, which surrounded a massive stone structure. She gave a little gasp of delight as Alex explained to her that the medieval tower covered with ivy dated back to the time of William the Conqueror and had been added onto by generation after generation until the house could not claim to be of any particular period.

"We're relatively new owners," he said with a smile. "The first Duke of Blakesley received both his title and the estate from Henry the Eighth. Old Rupert showed that he knew which side his bread was buttered on by giving his support to the king when he divorced Catherine of Aragon. He also persecuted the Catholics with great vigor, so I'm afraid we can't be proud of the method in which we obtained our inheritance."

He brought the surrey to a halt in the circular driveway and laughed at the awed expression on

Toria's face. "Don't you get lost?" she exclaimed. "How do you find your way about?"

"Oh, we've closed off a large portion of it, but when we were children that was not the case. What good times we had playing hide-and-seek in its dark corridors. Now as the owner, I find myself plagued by leaky roofs and drafty rooms that even huge fireplaces can't heat properly during the winter months."

Entering the great hallway, they knew tea was already in progress as the rise and fall of voices drifted down from the drawing room.

"Where is Alex?" It was a woman who asked the question in a loud, penetrating tone that rose above the others.

"He'll be along shortly with his guest for the weekend, a Miss Victoria Leighton," the duchess replied.

"Really, Marjorie," the woman continued, "I'm distressed to learn that we are spending a weekend in the company of an actress, and, far worse, a person who, I've been told, was once a chorus girl at the Alhambra."

Alex and Toria had reached the entrance to the drawing room, and he grasped her hand, holding her back, his face livid with anger. "Ignore Lady Charlotte," he urged in a low voice. "She has a vicious tongue but doesn't mean half of what she says."

Toria stood frozen in the doorway, her face paper white, her violet eyes dilated in horror, not so much from the insult she had received at the hands of Lady Charlotte, but by the sight of Viscount Covington leaning carelessly against the mantel, balancing a cup of tea in his hand.

To Toria the scene took on a nightmarish quality

as a tall, stately woman in a gray silk gown rose from the tea table, her hands outstretched in welcome. "My dear Miss Leighton," she said warmly. "Welcome to Uplands."

As she drew near, Toria saw that Alex had inherited his mother's dark, intelligent eyes and graceful movements. Before she could make any protest, she found herself propelled firmly across the drawing room and introduced to the other guests.

Toria was thoroughly upset by Lady Charlotte's cruel remarks, and the names and faces of the people she met became a blur until a familiar voice exclaimed, "Toria, how splendid to meet with you again!" She realized she was face to face with Lady Clara, who was addressing her as if she were an old friend instead of a servant in her mother's household.

"Lady Clara!" she managed to reply as her former mistress shook her hand and, smiling at her, said, "No, not Lady Clara—just Clara. Do come and sit by me so we can chat. There's so much I want to know about what has been happening to you lately. You'll never guess how I missed you when you left. I still do."

As Toria joined Lady Clara on a red velvet love seat in a far corner of the tremendous drawing room, she felt the rapid beating of her heart gradually slow down. She noticed that Lady Clara looked remarkably handsome and serene, perfectly turned out in an aquamarine lace gown.

"You look very well, milady," Toria ventured. "I heard of your marriage—" She paused, uncertain how Lady Clara felt today about her marriage to Lord Harrington, an alliance which she had tried so desperately to avoid.

"I'm happy, Toria," Lady Clara confided as if she had read Toria's thoughts. "Surprisingly so. Once I ceased rebelling, I discovered my husband and I possessed the ingredients to become, if not passionately in love, at least compatible. Now I am *enceinte*. Unfortunately a condition that rules out riding for the time being, but I'm willing to give that up for the joy of bearing a child. Isn't it strange how things eventually work out if you are patient?"

Impulsively Clara grasped Toria's hand and gave it an encouraging squeeze. "Tell me about yourself. What a courageous girl you were to strike out on your own. But then, I always knew you were too talented not to succeed. Remember the night when I had that beastly cold and you sang so beautifully for the Prince of Wales? I like to think that was the beginning of your career."

"It was, for I don't believe I realized until then that I had the ability to hold the attention of an audience."

The afternoon tea was drawing to a close as one by one the members of the party left to be escorted to their rooms.

Alone at last, with the door of her bedroom firmly closed and the servant girl, who had brought hot water for her bath, dismissed, she was still struggling to gain control of her storm-tossed emotions, to make a decision whether she should stay or leave immediately.

Although the scornful remarks uttered by Viscountess Covington still rang in her ears, they became secondary to the devastating shock of Piers's reentry into her life. The prospect of being forced to share a weekend in the country with him struck her as completely untenable.

She started when there was a gentle tap on her door, and composing herself with great difficulty, she called out, "Come in."

She was relieved to see that her visitor was the Duchess of Blakesley, for in her distraught state she had been fearful it might be Piers, pursuing her as he had in the past. Ever since their final parting, she frequently awoke in the middle of the night, haunted by a recurring dream: She was at Sutherland House, and he was chasing her along dark, narrow corridors, drawing nearer and nearer, taunting her for her foolishness in believing he would ever marry one of his mother's servants.

"My dear," her hostess began smoothly, closing the door behind her, "you're not dressed, and I did want to have a little chat with you before dinner." She was tall and stately in a black velvet gown relieved by only a string of luminous pearls. She was not a beautiful woman, Toria decided as she studied her face, but she had great character, with warmth and compassion in her brown eyes. Her smile reminded Toria of Alex.

"Well," the duchess continued easily, "I'll make my visit brief to give you time to prepare for the evening. I have completed a meeting with Lady Charlotte in which I informed her very candidly that any friend of my son's is most welcome in this house, and an insult will not be tolerated. I must apologize for a guest whose conduct was unpardonable."

"You are very kind," Toria replied in a tremulous voice.

"You were contemplating leaving?"

Toria managed the beginnings of a smile. "How did you guess?"

"It would be my first reaction. But don't leave, my dear. Don't leave. It would only serve to give Lady Charlotte satisfaction, and it would certainly be a grave disappointment to Alexander. I've been watching him here at Uplands all week, and if ever a man has displayed eagerness for a guest to arrive, he certainly has." She laughed, a musical, lilting laugh. "Since seeing you, I can understand why."

The duchess crossed over to her and laid a hand gently on her shoulder. "I have been looking forward to the opportunity for a talk with you, so I hope you won't leave and disappoint me. Promise me you will stay. You strike me as a young woman with enormous reserves of strength, and it would please me no end to have you show Lady Charlotte what the words *courage* and *character* really mean."

"I'll stay," Toria promised.

"Good!" Her manner became brisk and efficient. "Now I must see if the flower arrangements meet with my approval. We gather in the drawing room in thirty minutes."

The Duchess of Blakesley's thoughtful visit combined with her soothing words served to partially alleviate Toria's fears and anxieties. At least I'll stay until tomorrow, she decided. I'll simply ignore Piers's presence tonight. I imagine he'll be equally anxious to ignore mine. It's all in the past anyway. It happened a long time ago, when I was naïve and vulnerable. Surely by now I have the wisdom to handle such a weak and spineless creature.

As she selected a white chiffon gown from her wardrobe, a dress that Alex particularly admired, her confidence and normally high spirits returned. By the time she was ready to join the other guests in the drawing room, she was determined that nothing could destroy the pleasure of a weekend at Uplands with the man she would always love.

Chapter Thirty-Two

It was a relatively small house party, with only ten guests, as the duchess disliked to entertain hordes of people, preferring small groups who would be able to converse together in what she labeled "a civilized manner."

As they sipped their before-dinner sherry, Toria began to relax, actually enjoying herself. All the guests, with the exception of the Covingtons, went out of their way to be cordial. Apparently Lady Charlotte had not recovered from the sting of the duchess's reproof and was quite openly sulking, while Piers contributed little to the conversation. Toria had no way of knowing if that was his usual manner, or if he was as overwhelmed as she by this unfortunate encounter.

When they went in to dinner, she was relieved to see that Piers was seated at the other end of the table, some distance from her, but as it was a small gathering, inevitably their eyes met occasionally, and when they did, it seemed to Toria that his were morose and malevolent.

She found the conversation at dinner stimulating. Baron Selfridge sat on her right, a tremendous hulk of a man with a red face and heavy jowls. He began to question Alex about his recent trip to Paris.

"Tell me about the Eiffel Tower," he suggested. "What did you think of it?"

Alex laughed. "A monstrosity, but a marvelous achievement from an engineering point of view. I spent some time watching the workmen. It's a fascinating and rather awesome spectacle."

"What is the Eiffel Tower?" Toria asked with curiosity.

"It's a gigantic tower built of iron, which when completed in 1889 for the International Exhibition, will be nine hundred and eighty-four feet high. It will mark the one hundredth anniversary of the Fall of the Bastille."

The talk then turned to Africa—some of the guests arguing against so much money being poured into the colonies when there was great poverty at home, others defending the empire and extolling the virtues of the expansionists.

Toria, intrigued by the exchange, vowed to study more diligently the affairs of the world and said to Alex under her breath, "How can you possibly spend so much of your time with a silly, uneducated girl like me?"

He laughed. "There's more to life than travel and politics, and frankly I much prefer looking at you than at the baron. Besides, you're intelligent, and in no time at all you'll be as knowledgeable as anyone at this table."

As the dinner progressed, she discovered to her surprise and gratification that she was enjoying herself immensely, despite the presence of Piers and Lady Charlotte. When the Duchess of Blakesley, seated at the head of the table, gave her a conspiratorial smile of approval, she returned the smile, indicating with a graceful dip of her head that as far as she was concerned the crisis was over.

Alex, seated on her left, made a point of constantly including her in the conversation, his eyes reflecting his approval of her appearance.

"You look like a queen," he whispered once, lifting his glass of champagne in a silent toast, and she was glad she had worn her favorite gown of white chiffon and a sapphire necklace and bracelet she had recently purchased. Tonight her hair was swept high on her head, and in the glow of the candlelight, she was aware she had never appeared lovelier.

Toward the close of the meal, Baron Selfridge asked her if they would be honored later to hear her sing, and she replied, "Of course. I would be delighted to do so." For some months now she had been taking piano lessons and was able to accompany herself when she sang.

After the men enjoyed their port and the women made small talk in the drawing room, Toria sang the popular songs from the musical show in which she starred. She sang them directly to Alex—her way of communicating that she would always love him and that, no matter what the future held, nothing could ever change her abiding adoration.

When the guests settled down for an evening of bridge, she and Alex bowed out, and as the weather had become warm and pleasant, they strolled together through the beautiful formal gardens.

"What occurred this afternoon distressed me considerably, Victoria," Alex said.

"It distressed me also," she admitted. "I was on

the verge of leaving until your mother came to my rescue. While I was dressing for dinner, she persuaded me that it would be foolish to become overwrought over the incident. She's a very unusual person, Alex. I feel that under different circumstances we could become friends."

"I believe she considers herself already your friend. She told me before the guests arrived in the drawing room for dinner that she had reprimanded Lady Charlotte."

"Are they close friends?"

"Lady Charlotte's mother and mine have known each other all their lives. My mother feels sorry for Lady Charlotte. Her marriage has turned out to be a miserable one. I think she hoped that having Piers and Charlotte here together might improve their disintegrating relationship."

"He was anything but talkative during dinner."

Alex frowned. "He had already had more than enough to drink, and liquor puts him in an ugly mood. But, Toria, it is you who concern me. You're not regretting your visit to Uplands?"

She hesitated. "No, for I will always treasure the wonderful hours we shared this afternoon, although I must admit the prospect of meeting Caroline tomorrow has unnerved me. When will she arrive?"

"Early tomorrow morning. Her family's estate adjoins ours, and no matter how weary she is from her trip to Paris, she won't miss the hunt."

"Which I will not attend," Toria said with a laugh. "I'm not up yet to soaring over hedges and fording streams, so our confrontation won't occur until much later."

"You mustn't consider it a confrontation," he assured her. "Caroline is anxious to become your friend."

Toria shook her head slowly, puzzled that a man as cosmopolitan as Alex could honestly believe that two women in love with the same man could be at ease in each other's company.

"Don't be absurd, Alex," she said with a degree of asperity. "From what you've told me of your fiancée, I can't imagine she would be foolish enough to think that the hours you have spent at St. John's Wood were spent in the role of my protector, when it is obvious your obligations on that score ended some time ago."

"You forget one very important aspect," he replied calmly. "Caroline and I are not in love. Nevertheless, a marriage of convenience has its advantages, lacking such elements as anger and jealousy."

"And passion," Toria added. "Don't forget passion, Alex. Although apparently it is another element that you are willing to forgo."

"Don't, Victoria, don't spoil the short time we have left in each other's company."

They were standing on the terrace, leaning against the stone balustrade, when the moon, which had been obscured by a bank of clouds, was suddenly set free, bathing the lawns and gardens and outlining the delicate contours of Toria's face.

As Alex turned to her, about to plead once more for tolerance and understanding, he saw that she was crying. Finding himself unable to bear the thought of causing her anguish, he gathered her in his arms, kissing her tenderly at first until, finding himself consumed by waves of passion, his lips became urgent and demanding.

"My darling," she whispered clinging to him desperately. "It's been too long, far too long. Don't you agree?"

Brusquely he moved away from her. "Go inside, Victoria," he said in a harsh tone. "I beg you to obey me. You were right when you said the other day that we have no alternative but to part."

"Only because of your foolish pride, Alex," she cried out. "What can I say or do to make you realize how unwise it is to enter into a loveless marriage? You will regret it—very soon you will regret it, only to find it's far too late to make amends."

When he did not answer her, continuing to stare out at the moon-swept lawns, a cold, hard expression on his face, she left him. As she climbed the marble staircase to her room on the third floor, her overwhelming desire was to depart from Uplands that night or, at the very latest, the following morning. It would be an opportune time to leave, when most of the guests had joined the hunt.

Reaching her room, she began to toss her clothes helter-skelter into her empty suitcase until the words spoken by the Duchess of Blakesley earlier in the evening came back to haunt her. She had spoken of courage and of strength of character. Toria had been proud that Alex's mother believed she possessed such qualities. Certainly to run away from Uplands when Caroline and Alex were hunting would be anything but courageous, showing instead a lack of ability to accept defeat with dignity and grace.

Slowly unpacking her suitcase, she vowed with grim determination that she would never allow this small, charmed circle of the elite to suspect for one moment that she had been rejected by one of their members. Above all, she would never allow Alexander to know how deeply he had wounded her.

Chapter Thirty-Three

Toria was awakened very early the next morning as the members of the hunting party assembled in the courtyard beneath her bedroom window. Crossing to the window, she gazed at the vivid scene below—the gentlemen in their red coats, a stunning contrast to the ladies dressed in somber black. A liveried servant was passing the stirrup cup among them while the horses pranced, impatient to be off.

Toria recognized Lady Caroline at once. She was mounted on a gray horse which seemed unusually skittish, and as Toria watched Lady Caroline control her horse with ease, she recognized that Alex's fiancée was a superb equestrienne who would take any hedge, any fence without flinching. She was wearing a smart derby, her pale blond hair neatly tied back with a ribbon, the full skirt of her riding habit falling in graceful folds to the tip of her polished boots. An aristocrat through and through, Toria thought, wondering whatever had made her think she could successfully compete against her.

The master of the hunt raised his horn and, with a single blast, gave the signal that the hunt was about to begin. She caught her breath at the splendid sight as they rode out of the courtyard and galloped across the green lawns, the pack of hounds bounding along beside them, eager to pick up the scent of the fox.

A maid in a pink cotton dress tapped lightly on her door and entered carrying a metal tray with her morning cup of tea.

"Her Grace is having breakfast in the morning room, miss," she said. "She requests that you join her."

Selecting a blue-sprigged muslin frock, Toria dressed hurriedly, looking forward to meeting the Duchess of Blakesley again.

"There are only three of us left behind," the duchess said, giving Toria a warm smile as she entered. "As I understand Lady Clara is still sleeping, it gives you and me a chance to become better acquainted."

Wearing a frothy white peignoir, she lifted a silver pot and poured Toria a cup of tea. "Later, when they return from the hunt, there will be an enormous breakfast served in the dining hall. I hope you don't mind lighter fare now."

"Not at all." Toria accepted the proffered cup and, as she took a sip, was acutely aware that the duchess was studying her gravely.

"I had a lengthy talk with Alex last night," the duchess remarked. "He came to my suite after our guests had retired. Sometimes, you know, when a man inherits a dukedom at an early age, especially with a disposition as serious as Alex's, he is inclined to overemphasize his duties and obligations. Normally I go out of my way not to interfere in his life, but last night I felt it necessary to point out to him that lately he has become far too obsessed regarding his responsibilities. I also told him that I firmly believe in marrying for love."

"I caught a glimpse of Caroline in the courtyard this morning," Toria replied. "She's very beautiful, stately and poised. I can't blame Alex for considering her the perfect choice for his wife."

"Yes, except for a few most important factors. Alex is not in love with Caroline, or she with him, while it's quite clear that he is in love with you."

"Is it that obvious?" Toria asked, startled by the duchess's directness. "We thought we were successful in hiding our feelings last night."

The Duchess of Blakesley gave an amused chuckle. "My dear, believe me when I assure you that, despite your strivings, your regard for each other was extremely obvious—at least to me. Over the years I've learned to read my son's reactions like a book. He's head over heels in love with you, and as such a situation goes against his principles, his precepts, he is putting up a gallant fight, too gallant in my opinion. I told him so last night, and I also informed him that to me you possess all of the qualifications any duke could wish for in a wife."

"You're very kind." Toria's eyes filled with tears and she impatiently brushed them away.

"No, not kind, merely knowledgeable. Long ago I discovered that the most important ingredient in a marriage is love. I married for love. I never regretted it."

"Yet I doubt Alex will change his mind. He made it very clear to me on the terrace last night that he has no intention of doing so. After all, the wedding is only a few weeks away, which makes the situation even more complicated."

"We shall see," the duchess replied. "This is only Saturday morning. The house party does not end until Monday. Much can happen between now and then, but I want you to know, Victoria, that no matter what the outcome, I am on your side. I admire Lady Caroline. I always have. Certainly she has all the attributes to become a duchess. Nevertheless, I am extremely averse to my son entering into a loveless match. I have seen too many such alliances bring nothing but unhappiness to the parties involved."

There was no opportunity for a further exchange of confidences, as Lady Clara appeared in the doorway of the morning room. Toria, her mind in a whirlwind of contradictions, found it difficult to acknowledge that, yes, it was a fine day for the hunt, and yes, she had slept well the night before.

As she answered Lady Clara's questions automatically, she was thinking: Alex's mother not only knows we are in love, but she is willing to accept me as his wife. Her spirits soared to the very summit of joy, only to descend precipitously when she realized that there was no guarantee, no guarantee at all, that Alex would accept his mother's advice.

He was betrothed to Lady Caroline, and knowing all too well his stubborn pride, Toria was convinced that he would steadfastly continue to honor his commitment.

With a deep sigh she turned her flagging attention to Lady Clara and said, "Yes, do let's take a stroll through the gardens. In order to prepare ourselves for the hunt breakfast, we both need some exercise."

"It must be onerous for you not to be able to join the hunt," Toria remarked as she and Lady Clara walked sedately side by side along a brick path. "My fondest memory of you is seeing you return from a morning on horseback, full of high spirits from your ride."

"That's true. It is difficult to be housebound. But what about you? Why didn't you accompany them?"

Toria gave a rueful laugh. "Because I'm still classified as a novice, although Alex assures me I've made great progress."

Clara gave her an encouraging smile. "You'll soon learn. So Alex is your instructor?"

"Yes. We often ride together at my home in St. John's Wood."

"It's amazing to me, Toria, the way you have managed your life. How I admire your courage!"

"Some might call it foolhardiness," Toria replied, unable to keep a strain of bitterness out of her voice.

"You left Park Lane so suddenly," Lady Clara continued. "I've wondered often if it had anything to do with Piers."

Determined at all costs not to resurrect the unhappy events at Sutherland House, Toria shook her head vehemently. "No, Clara, Piers was not involved. I merely grew weary of my duties, and when we returned to London, it seemed an opportune time to leave. If I had continued on any longer, I might never have mustered the courage to depart."

"I've seen you several times at the Gaiety. You're wonderful, so extremely talented. But tell me, how did you happen to meet Alex? Everyone here is quite agog, you know, wondering why he invited you for the weekend. It's so out of character for Alex to—" She broke off, blushing and giving an embarrassed laugh. "I'm sorry, Toria," she finished. "Forgive me. I have no right to pry."

Although inwardly she was consumed with anger,

Toria held her head high, struggling to maintain her composure, admitting she should not find it surprising that Lady Clara was like all the rest of her class, unable to comprehend why a duke with an impeccable reputation would demean himself and ask an actress to spend a weekend at his country estate.

"Alex and I are friends, Lady Clara—nothing more. He was kind enough to help me when I needed help. Is that so impossible for you to understand?"

"No, no, of course not! Again please accept my apologies for being inquisitive. I couldn't help but feel last night during dinner how perfectly you and Alex complement each other. I'm extremely fond of him, Toria, and I'm equally fond of you. I should hate to see either of you hurt."

"Don't concern yourself about Alex or me. I have become an independent person, able to take the ups and downs without falling apart, while Alex is a mature, intelligent man who knows what he wants. After all, no one forced him to become betrothed to Lady Caroline. I imagine most of his friends consider him a very lucky man to have won her."

"On the surface it seems ideal, but I've never thought they were in love."

"You weren't in love when you married Lord Harrington, although now you appear to be happy and content."

"Yes, I am, but somehow my situation is a shade different. There was no one else I loved when I married Jamie, and he was not in love either. I am certain Alex adores you. I'm sure everyone at the house party is convinced of that!"

"You may be right," Toria replied, "although it appears, Clara, that love is not always enough to overcome family pride and loyalty to a woman who has already promised to be a man's wife. I find myself with only one avenue of escape. After this weekend is over, I intend to forget him. There is no other solution. I only trust that while here I do not become an embarrassment to him."

"You an embarrassment! Impossible!" Clara reached out her hand and pressed Toria's warmly. "Let me tell you this, Victoria Leighton. Any man who woos and wins you is most fortunate. If Alex is foolish enough not to recognize that, he deserves to lose you, and he'll regret it for the rest of his life. Indeed, I have half a mind to tell him so."

"Oh, don't, please don't!" Toria cried out. "It is up to Alex to make his own decisions. I know him well enough to realize that any advice might only serve to make him more adamant."

As they heard the beat of horses' hooves in the distance, Lady Clara Harrington gave Toria a sympathetic, understanding smile and turned in the direction of the house. "I promise I won't interfere," she said gently. "However, all weekend I will be praying that Alex will discover he can't exist without you."

That makes two of you on my side, Toria thought as she and Lady Clara walked briskly down the garden path. As the prospect of meeting Lady Caroline at the hunt breakfast was now imminent, she shivered despite the heat of the day and began to have second thoughts about her decision not to make a quick departure from Uplands.

Chapter Thirty-Four

The servants had risen long before dawn to prepare the elaborate hunt breakfast. By the time Clara and Toria reached the dining hall, the hunting party had already returned. Ravenous from their exhilarating ride through the countryside, they were demolishing the sumptuous array of food spread out on the long Sheraton table in the center of the room and on numerous sideboards along the walls.

Toria glimpsed Alex in the midst of a group of gentlemen who were gathered around a sparkling silver punch bowl. He seemed aware of her presence the moment she entered, for he broke off an exchange with Baron Selfridge to stare at her with a mixture of sadness and severity on his handsome face.

This is where he belongs, Toria thought. At Uplands, he epitomizes the country gentleman, thoroughly at home with his guests, without question the master of his great holdings, content to spend the rest of his life here, managing his estate and surrounding himself with friends and neighbors of the same background.

The women were clustered around the tables,

heaping their plates with the enticing delicacies that had been prepared for them. With a laugh Lady Clara urged Toria to join them. "These days," she explained, "I am constantly famished. Anyone would think I had been riding since daybreak instead of taking a leisurely stroll through the gardens."

Before Toria could reply, she felt a light tap on her shoulder and, turning around, found herself for the first time in the presence of Lady Caroline Stanley. She was impeccably attired, not a hair out of place, as if she had stepped out of a painting on some ancestral wall instead of returning from an arduous gallop on horseback. Her cheeks were still pink from the wind and the excitement of the chase, but it was her eyes that immediately captured Toria's attention. They were a pale blue, cold, remote, and unfriendly, although when she spoke, her voice was warm and pleasant.

"I've been eager to meet you, Miss Leighton," she said. "Alex speaks of you frequently. Tell me, are you enjoying your stay at Uplands?"

"Very much. How could I not? It is such a beautiful place."

"Isn't it? I am anxiously looking forward to the day when it will become my home. Alex has told you, I suppose, that we will be married within the month? I trust you will visit us occasionally." She threw Toria a challenging look, pressing her lips together in a thin, hard line.

"Occasionally perhaps," Toria replied, "but as I have a very demanding career, I rarely can find the time for a long country weekend." Toria was frowning, upset by the tone of the conversation, amazed that only last night Alex had reassured her that in a marriage of convenience one found neither anger nor jealousy. Either she loves him, Toria concluded, or she is so determined to become the Duchess of Blakesley that she has found it necessary to firmly and clearly establish her position to me. I wonder, could she possibly consider me a threat?

She was relieved when Alex approached them bearing a tray containing glasses of punch. He was either unaware of or chose to ignore the tension that permeated the dining hall, the fact that the animated rise and fall of many voices had dwindled and died, as every member of the hunting party became absorbed in the meeting of Lady Caroline and Toria.

"I'm glad you sought out Victoria, Caroline," he remarked easily. "I've been anxious for you two to meet."

"But I've seen Miss Leighton before, Alex. I guess it never seemed important enough to mention at the time, but during one of your excursions to Paris, I attended the Gaiety. I must say, you're a competent little actress, my dear. You must be, for musicals usually bore me to distraction."

Toria flushed, catching a flash of anger in Alex's eyes, although his response remained cool and detached. "Competence is hardly the correct word to express Victoria's talents," he remarked evenly. "She is remarkably endowed with all the attributes a great actress must possess."

"I'm sure she has a remarkable supply of all sorts of attributes," Lady Caroline retorted. "Both on and off the stage. Now if you will excuse me, Alex, I must mingle with your other guests." With a slight bow,

215

Caroline swept away, leaving them in an uneasy pool of silence.

"I must apologize—" Alex began awkwardly.

"Don't!" Toria broke in. "You should be relieved that your fiancée has some warm blood flowing in her veins and is not the lifeless, wooden figure you portrayed to me last night."

"Victoria, please!" Alex begged. "We mustn't quarrel. It is not only degrading but will destroy our friendship."

"Our friendship is already destroyed, my dear Alex," Victoria replied, her voice becoming as frosty as Lady Caroline's had been. "If you are so insensitive as not to realize this, I consider it a very good thing that you are entering into a marriage of convenience, for I don't believe you would be prepared to handle a marriage for love. Now, if you will excuse me, I too must mingle with the other guests."

With a mock bow, she left him still balancing the tray of punch glasses in his hands, a thoroughly disturbed and overwrought host.

"Bully for you!" Lady Clara whispered, drawing Toria to one side as she was about to join her and Lord Harrington. "Caroline can be a bitch, although I suspect it is the first time Alex has seen that side of her nature. She is determined to become a duchess, you see. You handled her magnificently—like Napoleon handled his troops at Waterloo."

Despite her anger, Toria burst out laughing. "But, Clara, Napoleon lost at Waterloo," she protested. "It was a disaster."

Lady Clara joined in her laughter. "History, I fear, has never been my strong point. I meant, of course, to say the Duke of Wellington."

216

The crisis at least temporarily over, the members of the hunting party resumed their animated conversation, intrigued that the weekend, instead of being boring and repetitive, appeared to be developing into a cause célèbre.

Chapter Thirty-Five

The Duchess of Blakesley had scheduled a ball for
Saturday night, inviting neighbors from the surrounding estates and engaging fiddlers from the village of Bedford to provide the music.

The dancing did not commence until well after ten
o'clock, for the dinner had been a lengthy one, twelve
courses in all, with additional guests present for the
occasion. Afterwards there had been the usual separation of the sexes, with the men, led by Alex, se-
questering themselves in the library, while the
women carried on an aimless conversation in the
drawing room.

At dinner Toria was grateful to discover that the
duchess had tactfully placed her between Baron Selfridge and Lord Harrington, far away from Laay
Caroline, who was seated next to her fiancé. Alex, as
master of the household, presided at the foot of the
long table.

To her surprise Jamie Harrington proved to be an
amusing dinner companion, regaling her with hilari-
ous stories of previous hunts, where the sly fox
proved to be smarter than the most dedicated eques-
trians in England, more often than not outwitting
them in the end. Baron Selfridge, a rather gruff and

red-faced gentleman, also engaged her attention, openly admiring her appearance, which helped to diminish the debilitating effect of the bitter exchange with Lady Caroline during the hunt breakfast.

Toria had dressed for the evening with extreme care, determined to take second place to no one, especially not to Lady Caroline. Suspecting that Alex's fiancée would wear virginal white to emphasize the fact that she was soon to become a bride, Toria selected a violet satin gown that brought out the highlights of her magnificent golden hair and made her violet eyes more mysterious and secretive than ever.

Wishing to appear young and vulnerable instead of mature and stately, she had allowed her hair to fall in soft waves around her shoulders. Her only jewels were a delicate diamond necklace with matching bracelet, one of many gifts Alex had brought back to her from Paris.

"Lady Caroline looks every inch the duchess tonight," Jamie Harrington remarked a trifle sarcastically as the soup plates were removed and replaced by the fish course.

Taking a sip of chilled Chablis, Toria was forced to admit that she certainly did, and that she had been correct in assuming Caroline would wear white. Her pale blond hair was piled high on her head, crowned by a diamond tiara that glimmered in the candlelight. She was surveying the scene around her with an imperious air, bestowing regal smiles on the assembled guests, except for Toria whom she gazed at only once briefly, without a flicker of recognition.

Only half listening to Baron Selfridge's rendition of a long and tedious account of a recent painful siege of gout, she noted that Piers had been placed directly across from her. She was relieved to see that he was so engaged in consuming such prodigious quantities of wine that he seemed unaware of her existence. At least that is one unfortunate experience that is in the past, she thought, and soon this painful weekend in the country will be in the past too. In time it will fade away completely.

Commiserating with Baron Selfridge over his considerable number of maladies, as he progressed from the gout to detailed descriptions of rheumatism, migraines, and bronchitis, she breathed a sigh of relief when the lady on the other side of the baron began a lively exchange on the morning's hunt, which commanded all of his attention.

When Lord Harrington launched into a discussion of a recent trip to Italy, against her volition her eyes were drawn to Alex's end of the table. Although his head was bent toward Lady Caroline as he politely replied to one of her remarks, his eyes were fastened on Toria, and she read in them remorse and despair.

Startled when Lord Harrington remarked, "Alex appears to be anything but a happy future bridegroom," she shrugged her shoulders and said with studied indifference, "Prewedding jitters, I imagine."

"Or prewedding second thoughts!" Jamie added with a laugh. "I agree with my intuitive wife that you and he were meant for each other."

Unable to come up with an adequate response, Toria smiled at him and said gently, "Now do tell me more about Italy. I've never had the good fortune to travel there."

The ballroom ran the length of the main house. Tonight it had been transformed into a magical place with a thousand candles in crystal chandeliers, creating an ethereal atmosphere, while against the white and gold walls marble urns had been placed filled with crimson roses.

White and gold programs were issued to the ladies, and Toria's card was immediately commandeered by the baron and returned to her with every dance taken. She saw Alex's name scrawled halfway down the list and noted with considerable relief that Piers was not to be one of her partners. In fact, after searching the room for him, she discovered that he was not present. She wondered if he had consumed so much wine and brandy that he had become too unsteady to put in an appearance.

It was the fifth dance and Alex claimed it. Later, looking back, Toria wondered if the outcome would have been different if it had been a mazurka instead of a valse.

He approached her with a formal bow as the instruments struck up the first notes of the dance. He was splendid in his black evening clothes with a white frilly shirt to relieve the somberness of his apparel.

They did not speak as his arm encircled her slender waist. They moved at first slowly and then swiftly over the polished parquet floor. Toria knew that all eyes were upon them as they whirled faster and faster in perfect rhythm to the fiddlers' romantic melody.

As the last note of the valse ended, Alex grasped her arm and propelled her out onto a balcony which overlooked the gardens. It was a dark night. Clouds had rolled in, obscuring the moonlight, and the only sound was the gentle splash of a fountain beneath them and the muted voices and laughter of the guests in the ballroom.

"I love you, Victoria," he said without preamble. "I cannot lose you." As he spoke the words she had been yearning to hear for so long, his arms were about her, drawing her close to him as they were lost in a tidal wave of desire. "Never leave me, my darling," he murmured. "I will speak with Caroline tonight and beg her to release me."

"But will she?" Toria whispered.

"She must. I'm certain that she, like everyone else at the ball, is aware we were fated for each other. My mother told me so last night. Those were her very words—fated for each other. I was still too stubborn, too foolish to acknowledge that she was speaking the truth."

"My, my." Caroline's cool voice broke the spell between them. "What a charming scene. Tell me, Alex, when we marry, do you intend to continue such clandestine interludes? When we became betrothed, I pledged to be faithful to you. Naturally, I assumed I could always count on your loyalty and support."

Toria attempted to break away from Alex, but he continued to hold her close in his arms. "I apologize, Caroline," he said stiffly. "When I asked for your hand in marriage, I had yet to meet Victoria. When we met, as you well know, the idea of falling in love with her never entered my mind, but fall in love I did. Despite my efforts to honor my commitment to you, I find it has become impossible. I was about to seek you out tonight and ask you to forgive me, to release me from our betrothal."

Lady Caroline laughed harshly. The lights from

the ballroom outlined her face, which was as cold and hard as marble. "I was content to marry you, Alex, as you were apparently content to marry me. Since childhood, it always seemed the correct, the expected course to take. Now I find myself reluctant to contemplate an alliance with a man who has suddenly changed from a steadfast suitor to a man who can be easily cuckolded by a chit who arose from the gutter. You are free to do as you wish, but since I resent being further humiliated, I am leaving this instant for Stanley Hall. If you recover your senses, call on me."

Before Alex could reply, she swung about and reentered the ballroom.

"Oh, Alex," Toria moaned, "I'm so sorry to be the cause of such a scene."

"Don't be sorry, my darling," he said tenderly, still holding her close. "Caroline has every right to be angry, but that soon will pass, for she is young and lovely and will find another man more able than I to give her happiness. She is clever enough to realize that under the circumstances our life together would be empty and meaningless—a sham."

He kissed her again, a deep, lingering kiss. "Now go to your room, my sweet. Tomorrow and all the days thereafter will be yours and mine. We will marry soon, very soon. I promise you."

As he released her at last with a final tender kiss, Toria sped on wings of bliss through the ballroom and up the grand staircase to her room. Her feet seemed to barely touch the marble floors.

Chapter Thirty-Six

Reaching the seclusion of her bedchamber, Toria closed the door swiftly behind her, leaning against it and breathing heavily, unable to fully accept the dramatic scene on the balcony which had changed the course of three lives.

Despite the fact that it had been Caroline who had thrown down the gauntlet, establishing them as adversaries, she experienced a pang of regret that Lady Caroline must now face the humiliation of a broken engagement.

This regret was soon replaced by great waves of happiness that swept over her at the knowledge that Alex had asked her to marry him, at last conquering his stubborn pride. She knew it would take time to adjust to the shock of emerging the winner, for at dinner she had conceded defeat as she had watched Lady Caroline play the role of Alex's future wife with such consummate skill.

Elated but exhausted, she undressed hurriedly. Slipping into a filmy nightgown and seating herself at the dressing table, she began to brush her luxuriant hair. Suddenly her bedroom door burst open with a crash. She swung about, appalled to see Piers framed in the doorway. It was obvious he had had far too much to drink, for he was weaving as he stepped across the threshold.

"You little bitch," he muttered. "I'll never forgive you for the trick you played on me."

She gave him a pitying glance, revolted that she had ever felt the slightest bit in love with him, that once long ago she had craved his caresses. Now, as he stood before her, she saw him exactly as he was—a rather stupid young man, arrogant, spoiled, and extremely shallow.

"And what you did to me was of no consequence?" she asked in a tone of utter contempt. "You may be a viscount, Piers, but you will never be a gentleman. That old crone, satiated with gin, was admirably suited for the likes of you."

With an oath, he stumbled toward her, and jerking her roughly to her feet, gripped her shoulders in a tight vise.

"I detest you," she screamed, struggling to escape from his embrace, but he was too strong for her to combat. Kissing her brutally, he forced her toward the bed.

Flinging her onto the silken sheets, he bent over her, his hands still on her shoulders starting to rip off her gown. She continued to fight desperately, clawing at his face with her fingers, horrified that the old nightmare of his pursuit of her was becoming a reality.

Realizing that she had no chance against his superior strength, she opened her mouth to scream again, but before she could utter a sound, his hands covered her lips. "Be quiet," he said fiercely. "Once you begged for my embraces. You couldn't have enough of them. I'm willing to wager that Alex can't answer your needs as well as I."

On the verge of fainting, she closed her eyes, sickened by the expression of naked desire on his flushed face. Then suddenly, miraculously, she was free of him. Strong hands pulled him away from her, and she saw that Alex was her rescuer. Pinning Piers's arms behind his back, Alex tossed him toward the door where he collapsed like a rag doll across the threshold.

"Get out before I kill you," Alex said. There was no doubt in Toria's mind that if Piers hadn't stood up unsteadily and scuttled away, his life would have been in imminent danger.

"Are you all right?" Alex asked anxiously as she pulled herself slowly to an upright position.

"Yes, thanks to you," she answered and began to sob from the sheer relief that Piers was gone and she was safe.

"Stay there. I'll return shortly. I'm getting some brandy." Reassured that she had suffered no injury, he smiled for the first time and added drily, "We both need it."

As she lay on the bed, still half-dazed, she realized that she was wearing only a flimsy nightgown, which had been torn, exposing her breasts. With a great effort she struggled to her feet and put on a white satin robe. Still shaken by Piers's brutal attack, she began to shiver uncontrollably despite the warmth of the night.

Alex returned to find her standing in the center of the room, no longer crying, her face a frozen mask of horror and despair.

"Here, take this, Toria," Alex urged, pressing a

glass into her hand. With shaking fingers she clutched it and raised it to her lips.

"You were prepared to kill him," she whispered.

"Without a doubt." He stood before the hearth, glass in hand, extremely handsome in a black velvet dressing gown. "My room is not far down the hallway. Thank God I heard the ruckus. I thought you were having a bad dream until I reached your door and saw the swine actually attempting to violate you —and almost succeeding."

"I've dreamed of it happening so often that at first I believed it was a dreadful nightmare."

"Tell me, Victoria," he asked, "have you known Piers before this? Was he the man you ran away from in the garden that night at Sutherland House? Although he is noted for being a scoundrel, I can't believe he would attack a woman he had just met. What is your connection with him? I desperately desire your answer."

She finished the brandy and joined him by the fireplace, looking deeply into his troubled eyes. "It was when I worked for the Esterbrooks," she began. "For a time I believed I was in love with him. It was foolish of me, I know, but then I was very young and foolish."

"Are you telling me that Piers was once your lover?"

She replied after a long silence, her voice so low that he could barely make out the words. "No—but I believed we were betrothed, that he desired to marry me."

"Did you permit that rake to take any liberties with you?" he demanded, his eyes widening in astonishment, his laugh harsh and bitter. "If so, my dear

Victoria, all I can say is that the joke's on me. Since we first met, I have looked upon you as a pure and virtuous woman, denying myself an intimate relationship with you, which, incidentally, I greatly desired. Therefore, if you have bestowed your favors on that wretch, as far as I am concerned I never wish to see you again."

"Please, Alex, you must hear me out." She spoke pleadingly, frightened by the sarcasm in his voice. "I was never Piers's mistress, but, yes, we did kiss and embrace. I promised to elope with him."

His face flushing with anger, Alex poured himself a second glass of brandy and flung himself into a chair. "So tonight I had the dubious honor of asking for the hand of one of Viscount Covington's discarded wenches."

"That's a rotten way to put it," she cried out, her eyes flashing with fury. "It seems to me, Alex, you are being both pompous and overbearing. If you have such little faith and trust in me, what kind of a future could we have together?"

"I've been thinking the same thought," he replied coldly. "It was foolish of me to lose my head tonight and ask to become betrothed to you, for a woman who has been held in Covington's arms could never be my wife."

Wearily, she crossed over to him and placed a hand on his shoulder. It was a pleading gesture, begging him to accept what she had told him. "I can't say anything more, Alex. If you are determined to think ill of me, how can I convince you of my innocence? What more can I do to justify myself?"

"There is nothing you can do to justify yourself," he replied. Standing up abruptly, he drew her to him, and in his eyes she saw the same desire that Piers's eyes had held a short time ago.

"But you could become my mistress," he continued, "for if you have willingly allowed one man to make love to you, why not another? I have been patient and understanding and honorable for far too long. I think you owe it to me to grant me your favors."

"If you wish it, Alex," she said tearfully. "If you wish it—take me here and now."

Crushing her to him, his lips found hers in a bruising kiss, and as he made a move to pick her up in his arms, he felt against his cheek the hot tears which were coursing down her face. "You are crying!" he exclaimed. "Why?"

"For what we've lost," she sobbed. "For what we shared the other day when we rowed across the pond. For what we pledged to each other tonight on the balcony. It has been lost forever.

"Yes, I was stupid when I believed Piers's offer of marriage, but I was far more stupid when I met you and judged you to be something that I now know you are not. It is clear you never loved me. Otherwise in your heart there would be forgiveness."

He was no longer holding her in his arms but was moving away from her, striding toward the door. "Too much has happened tonight," he said. "I find I have lost my desire to make love to you. Perhaps by morning we can reach a calmer plateau, discuss more rationally what our next step should be." Without a backward glance, he was gone.

To her the confrontation with Piers had become secondary. Alex's reaction had become of primary importance. At first he had been skeptical, but was soon convinced that she was a wanton. The affinity which had existed between them had dissolved into nothingness. In his eyes she had become merely another available woman, to be had for an evening or two with the tacit understanding that the affair was tenuous, without substance.

As the night wore on, she reproached herself bitterly for ever having imagined it could have ended differently. In his estimation, he now considers me one step above a strumpet, she thought. Crossing to the writing desk and finding pen and paper, she wrote him a letter.

"Alex"—she wrote—"It is clear that you do not love me. If you did, nothing could destroy your trust in me. What have we to discuss in the morning? The decision was made when I saw the scorn in your eyes. When you read this letter, I shall be gone. I am asking, no, I am demanding that you do not attempt to see me again. Toria."

She did not sleep that night. Stealing out of the silent house at daybreak, she aroused a stableboy who agreed to drive her to Bedford. Drained of all emotion, she returned to London and then on to St. John's Wood.

Chapter Thirty-Seven

St. John's Wood was too replete with memories for Toria to linger there for any length of time. She found herself far too distressed to attempt to explain to Ann why she had cut short her weekend in the country, while her aunt, susceptible to her moods, refrained from asking questions.

Everywhere she went on the property reminded her of Alex—the bridle paths through the woods, the gardens where they had strolled on pleasant days, a table they had purchased one winter's afternoon at Sotheby's, the Renoir in the drawing room which he had brought back from one of his trips to Paris.

All these reminders were of such a painful nature that in less than twenty-four hours she resolved that, at least for a while, she must go away. Perhaps unfamiliar surroundings would help to dim her haunting memories. She broached the subject to Ann the day after her return from Uplands.

"Where will you go?" Ann asked.

"Where else but the theater? The musical is closing, but I think I could manage to join some road company touring the provinces. I need work and a change of scenery. St. John's Wood holds far too many memories for me."

"And Alex—do you intend to leave Alex too?" Ann ventured with a troubled glance.

"Alex and I are no longer friends. Don't ask me for the reasons, Ann. I can't bear to discuss them. Maybe someday you'll know the full story, but not now."

The mere fact she had reached a decision gave her some measure of solace. Traveling to London on the following day, she had no difficulty signing up as a member of a company that was already journeying through northern England.

"Mostly one-night stands, Miss Leighton," her agent warned her as she signed the contract without even glancing at the terms. "Are you certain it is what you want? They'll be extremely glad to acquire a singer of your stature, of course, but I must admit to some surprise that you're interested."

"They need a singer; I need to work. It's as simple as that," Toria replied tersely. "When should I leave?"

"They'll be in Liverpool on Thursday—a three day engagement there. Rather short notice, I fear."

"Not at all. That gives me ample time."

With a quick handshake, she departed, leaving behind a puzzled man, who found it difficult to comprehend why Miss Victoria Leighton, the most valuable piece of property he had acquired in years, was willing, even eager, to go on tour during the summer months with a second-rate company that was barely able to meet its payroll.

It was Wednesday. On the brink of tears, Toria stood in the entrance hall, dressed in her traveling cloak and bonnet. Turning to Ann for one last embrace, she said in a low, tense voice so that the ser-

232

vants would not overhear, "You must tell no one, especially Alex, where I have gone. It's a closed chapter which I have no wish to reopen. I promise to write you frequently, and you mustn't worry about my safety." They clung together for a few moments longer before she climbed into her carriage and, with a wave of her hand, departed.

To Toria, Liverpool proved to be a dismal, uninspiring seaport town. The theater where the road company was playing was situated on a dilapidated side street, not far from the busy harbor. Their hotel was equally shabby, and she suspected that it also housed women of ill repute.

Under normal conditions, Toria would have been appalled by the conditions under which she was expected to work, but instead she considered the change from the beauty and luxury of Uplands a welcome relief. At least, she decided, there is nothing here to remind me of the past. She smiled bitterly as she thought of how dismayed the Duke of Blakesley would be if he were forced to enter such a sleazy environment.

He'll never find me here, she decided. Not that I believe for one moment he has the slightest intention of searching for me. Her spirits plummeted as she pictured him riding on horseback to Stanley Hall to plead with Lady Caroline to forget the unpleasant country weekend and renew their former relationship, as if their engagement had never been broken.

To her surprise she found the members of the company warm and receptive. She suspected they hoped her presence would serve to stimulate the lagging ticket sales at the box office.

Thursday night their audience increased considerably. Friday night was close to a sellout, and the manager was elatedly predicting that on Saturday there would be standing room only for the evening performance. Cleverly he had arranged for Toria to appear three times on stage to sing her romantic ballads—at the beginning, the middle, and the finale —this way assuring himself that the audience would stay throughout in anticipation of her future appearances.

A dedicated artist, Toria gave as much of herself in Liverpool as she had at the Gaiety in London, where she had grown accustomed to performing before the royal family and members of the aristocracy. She was surprised to discover that she felt more pleasure singing to an audience who had sacrificed to purchase a ticket than to the idle rich, who often arrived at the theater so satiated with food and wine that it took great skill to arouse and sustain their enthusiasm.

By Saturday evening she had convinced herself that this way of life was the answer to her problems and that in time it would serve to lessen her yearning for Alex. In fact, she had reached the conclusion that when the summer engagement was concluded, she would sell her home in St. John's Wood, never to return to a place that had failed dismally to bring her even the remotest measure of happiness.

Chapter Thirty-Eight

The Duke of Blakesley had awoken on the morning after Toria's departure from Uplands to overcast skies and the promise of rain. He lay in bed for some time, depressed and unwilling to preside as host at a house party that, instead of being pleasurable, had become repugnant to him. Lethargically he arose and strode to the window, his worst thoughts confirmed that it would be a gloomy, dismal day, when he parted the curtains and saw streaks of rain slashing against the mullioned panes.

What would he say to Toria, he pondered? How would he entertain his guests, who by now would undoubtedly be restless and bored? How would he explain Lady Caroline's abrupt departure, and how would his mother react to the events of last night, one following so quickly on the heels of another? The entire situation was completely out of control.

With horror the picture of Piers struggling with Victoria, attempting and almost succeeding in ravishing her, rose once more to the forefront of his mind. All night long the scene had constantly haunted him, and he was still appalled by the fact that the woman whom he had asked to become his wife had confessed to him that once she had loved Viscount

235

Covington, that once she had consented to be his bride.

Rejecting Victoria, determined this very morning to sever their relationship, Alex turned to consider the question of Lady Caroline. Her behavior yesterday had been a grave disappointment to him. Both at the hunt breakfast and at the ball, she had displayed all of the earmarks of a fishwife. To his great surprise her mask of serenity and poise had deserted her. Did she love him, after all? Was that the reason for her surprisingly forceful reaction to finding Victoria in his arms? Or was she perhaps merely disappointed when confronted with the possibility of not becoming the Duchess of Blakesley? He sighed deeply, a thoroughly disturbed man, faced with a multitude of problems. He would have to deal with Piers too, he realized. He could not allow such a brutal act to occur under his roof without throwing the rascal out.

Delaying the moment when he must face such unpleasant situations, he took a bath, dressed leisurely, and ate breakfast in his room. Then, unable to postpone some sort of positive action any longer, he reluctantly left his suite.

In the corridor he was accosted by one of the maids, who with a formal curtsey delivered Toria's message. His reaction to it was mixed—sorry that she had decided to leave, yet to a certain extent relieved. He had convinced himself during his sleepless night that, as there was no future for the two of them, he must face the unpleasant task of telling her so. Now at least that task could be postponed.

Descending to the morning room, he found only one member of the house party present. It was Baron

Selfridge, in such a blue funk that he had substituted coffee and buttered toast for his usual hearty breakfast of eggs, bacon, and kippers.

"It's all been very upsetting, my dear fellow," the Baron sputtered.."Never in my years of experience have I ever seen a country weekend disintegrate so rapidly. First, last night, without a word of explanation, Lady Caroline departs for Stanley Hall. Followed this morning by Lord Piers and Lady Charlotte, who even forgo breakfast, muttering about some extreme emergency at home. Most disturbing of all, I understand Miss Leighton has also departed, before dawn I've been told. No one apparently knows why she made such a precipitous flight. It's all so disconcerting that I think I too should be on my way."

"Please reconsider, Benjamin," Alex replied, making an enormous effort to appear relaxed and at ease. "It looks as if we are saddled with a rainy day, so why don't we engage in a game of billiards?"

They repaired to the game room where Alex, to his mortification, found he was so distraught that for the first time in their many engagements, he was handily defeated by the baron.

"A bit off your game, what?" Baron Selfridge commented with a twinkle in his eye. "Imagine I'd react the same if such a charming lady as Miss Leighton up and left me in the middle of the night. I hope for your sake, Alex, everything eventually works out to your satisfaction. Damned fine woman, Miss Leighton! I'd marry her myself if she would have an old duffer like me!"

Receiving no response from the duke, the baron cleared his throat several times, turned a fiery red, and suggested going to the library for a spot of brandy. Over the years he had learned that a convivial drink by an open fire more often than not solves what beforehand appeared to be an unsolvable problem.

To Alex the day became endless and frustrating as he struggled to entertain his remaining guests, who had no intention of departing until Monday and were consumed with curiosity as to what had actually occurred during the ball the night before.

Not until late Monday afternoon, when the last carriage had finally departed, did Alex and his mother find themselves alone at Uplands.

"I suggest a sherry in the drawing room, Alex," the Duchess of Blakesley said crisply. "I am not only very concerned about Victoria's unexpected departure, but also I can't overlook the sudden departure of several of our other guests. Please, if you can, enlighten me."

Feeling like a schoolboy who had carelessly blotted his copybook, Alex poured sherry for himself and his mother. Then, standing with his back to the fire, he said brightly, hoping to avoid a frank discussion, "Have you noticed that the skies are clearing? I expect tomorrow will be a lovely day."

The duchess brushed aside his prognosis of the weather impatiently. "Why did Victoria Leighton leave?" she demanded.

"I found her in her bedroom with Piers," he replied in a low, tense voice.

"Surely the meeting was not of her own volition," the duchess responded quickly. "I know Piers—we all do. He can't resist a beautiful woman. I refuse to

238

believe that she willingly gave him access to her bed-chamber."

"No, not willingly. I'm certain of that. Nevertheless, I have learned that when she was a servant at the Esterbrooks', she fell in love with him."

"Which is not surprising! I can readily see how a young, naïve girl like Victoria might be smitten by Piers. It is obvious to me that your reaction to the episode must have been overly violent, otherwise why would Victoria have fled from Uplands in the middle of the night? I trust, Alex, indeed I pray, you were not too harsh with her. However, observing the expression on your face, I fear you were. What a pity! Now, if you will please tell me—why did Lady Caroline rush off in the midst of the ball without the courtesy of an explanation?"

"She stumbled upon Victoria and me on the balcony. I was asking Victoria to be my wife. Naturally, Caroline was most upset."

"Naturally!" There was a note of sarcasm in the Duchess of Blakesley's voice. "Alex, I must say that for an intelligent man—and I have up until now considered you intelligent—you have handled this entire situation most ineptly. I've surmised for some time that you love Victoria. Meeting her this weekend, I realized at once how right she is for you. Long ago, you should have explained your plight to Caroline, but no, you were too foolish to do so. Instead you set up ridiculous barriers like family pride and loyalty to prevent a union which anyone can see was meant to be. Good for Victoria! I'm glad she bolted from such an impossible situation. Don't you have the slightest conception of the courage it took for her to come here this weekend? It obviously disturbs

239

you, my dear son, to know that she is illegitimate and an actress to boot, but let me tell you, it does not disturb me—not one whit. So, due to your false pride, it appears you have lost her. I'm inclined to believe you deserve to lose her. The poor child! Attacked by that wastrel Piers, needing your love and support and instead receiving scorn and abuse. Well, she's gone. You rejected her, and now I suppose you'll return to Caroline."

"No, never to Caroline."

"You plan to continue in your bachelor state?"

Alex, overwhelmed by his mother's strong reaction to the affair, thoroughly accustomed to obtaining her instant support and sympathy, replied coldly, "Yes, I do, since the woman I love has proven to be unworthy of me, and the woman who is worthy of me, I do not love. I see no other recourse."

He finished his sherry, placed the crystal glass on a table, and with a stiff bow left the drawing room.

The duchess remained seated by the fire, an expression of satisfaction on her face. "My words will haunt him," she said softly to the empty room. "Soon, with any luck, he will recognize the folly of his ways and run to Victoria's side. I can only hope that when he does it will not be too late!"

Chapter Thirty-Nine

When faced with a problem in the past, Alex had usually ridden around his estate, finding that such activity served to restore his spirits and give him a measure of tranquillity. This time even an exhausting gallop of several hours' duration failed to mitigate the uneasy feeling that he had overreacted to the scene in Victoria's bedroom and might very well spend the rest of his life regretting the harsh words that had caused her to flee from Uplands. His mother's response to the incident, the scorn in her voice when she had upbraided him, also rested uneasily on his conscience.

By Wednesday evening, unable to endure any longer the Duchess's aloofness toward him, he announced that he was departing for London early the following morning and had no notion when he might return. She accepted his decision without comment, which served to make him even more uncomfortable.

Arriving in the city, he went directly to his town house in Belgrave Square, only to find the atmosphere there as depressing as it had been at Uplands. He had hoped that in a house where Victoria had never been, his memories of her might lessen, but as he paced through the silent rooms, he became increasingly restive.

On Friday afternoon he ordered his carriage and drove to St. John's Wood, having concluded during a disquieting night, when sleep continued to elude him, that at least he owed Victoria some sort of apology. After all, he had invited her to Uplands in the first place, and his acrimonious words had caused her to leave.

Deciding that as her host he must make amends for any discourtesy, he spent the entire journey from London deliberating as to what he would say to her and wondering what her reaction to his apology might be.

Therefore it was a bitter blow when he arrived to learn that Victoria was not at home. It was Sophie, opening the front door, who informed him that she hadn't the slightest clue regarding Miss Leighton's whereabouts.

Confronting Ann, who was working in her herb garden, he received a similar answer. "I'm very sorry, Alex, but Toria made me promise not to disclose her whereabouts," Ann explained in a troubled voice. No cajoling on his part succeeded in breaking down her resistance.

Returning to London, he went to his club for dinner, determined to avoid at all costs another evening alone at Belgrave Square. In his distraught state, it seemed to him that the servants were tiptoeing about as if there had been a death in the family.

Shunning the conviviality of the bar, he went directly to the deserted reading room, ordering a whiskey and soda along with a copy of the London *Times*. To his disgust he discovered that not even an article on a recent lively debate in the House of Commons could capture his attention. Turning to the theatrical section and noting that the musical at the Gaiety had closed, he was eagerly scanning the page, hoping for some mention of Victoria, when a heavy hand clapped him on the shoulder. With a scowl, he heard Baron Selfridge's gruff voice welcoming him back to London.

"You look a mite peaked, Alex," the baron said. "Perhaps what you need is another drink." Ringing the bell for service, Benjamin Selfridge settled down in a leather chair opposite the duke.

"I'm fine," Alex replied in a cool, clipped tone which indicated quite clearly that he was not in the mood for company.

"That's good to hear," the baron responded blandly. "Although I must say you don't sound convincing."

When Alex did not answer, Benjamin Selfridge lit a cigar with great deliberation and cleared his throat, making no move to leave a friend who quite obviously did not welcome his presence. "I've just come from the bar," he continued, "where I picked up an intriguing piece of information. Thought I'd pass it along to you for what it's worth. Funny, but ever since the weekend I've been puzzling over why Miss Leighton left Uplands so abruptly. Now, I believe, I have the answer."

"You have?" Alex asked, his voice expressing complete indifference.

"Yes, I believe I have. You know Sonny Wilkinson, of course. He returned this afternoon from a trip to Liverpool and mentioned in passing that Miss Leighton was appearing there—with some rather undistinguished road company. Strange, don't you think? But then, I suppose, once the theater is in your blood, you can't stay away from it for any length of time. I suspect you know the musical she was in at the Gaiety has closed. I couldn't help but observe what you were reading. Undoubtedly she left Uplands in order to rehearse. Don't you agree?"

"Undoubtedly."

Baron Selfridge finished his drink and stood up slowly, wincing slightly. "My blasted gout," he groaned. "As I can see you are not in a talkative mood, old chap, I'll toddle back to the bar."

Alex gave him an abstracted nod. When the baron disappeared from view, he hurriedly placed his untouched drink on a nearby table, tossed the London *Times* aside, and strode out of the reading room.

Ordering his carriage, he urged the driver to return as speedily as possible to Belgrave Square. There is a slim chance I can catch the night train to Liverpool, he thought, this time admitting to himself that he wanted to find Victoria, not to apologize for the disastrous country weekend, but to tell her of his abiding love and beg her to become his wife.

Chapter Forty

As the manager had predicted, on Saturday night there was not a vacant seat in the house, with a line of people outside the theater hoping to gain admittance. At the end of her first performance, Toria returned to her dressing room elated by the enthusiastic reception she had received, and thankful she had been astute enough to recognize that hard work was her only salvation.

Entering the shabby room to which she had been assigned, she halted, her eyes fastened on a white box that had been placed on her dressing table. She stared at it for several moments before gaining the courage to lift the cover and peer inside. With trembling fingers she touched the single red rose which lay in a bed of delicate green ferns. Slowly she removed the coroneted card with the name of the Duke of Blakesley engraved upon it and read his message. Very brief, it simply said: "I love you."

The card fell from her listless fingers to the floor. Why can't he stay out of my life? she asked herself fiercely. Why must I suffer another hour in his presence listening to his gentlemanly apologies and the tiresome list of reasons why, although he loves me, we cannot marry?

Her eyes flashing, she threw the red rose angrily on the floor, grinding it under her foot. Leaving her room, she informed the startled doorman that he was not to allow anyone, no matter how important he might be, to gain admittance to her dressing room. When the time came for her next appearance, she was amazed that she was able to continue as if nothing had occurred, assured by the tremendous ovation at the conclusion of the evening that her singing had been more provocative, more heartrending than ever before.

She remained in her dressing room long after her final curtain call, determined not to leave until the entire cast had departed, as well as the stage-door Johnnies. When there was a light tap on her door, she did not answer it. As the door swung slowly open, she was standing in front of the mirror, fastening her evening cape. Without turning, she said in an unsteady voice. "I don't wish to see you, Alex."

"But I'm not Alex, whoever he might be!"

Swinging about, she saw Willie Sloan, a middle-aged comedian in the company. He was standing hesitantly on the threshold. "You look as if you could use a drink," he said quietly.

She studied him seriously for a long moment. Since joining the company, she had found him to be a kindly man, admired by every member of the cast. At this low point in her life, she grasped at his invitation as if he had thrown her a lifeline.

"It's only a short walk," he said with a smile, "to a small, cozy pub where we can celebrate your great success."

Wordlessly, she walked with him along the darkened corridors, hesitating at the stage door. As if he

246

sensed her intention to avoid an unwelcome encounter, he said, "It's all right. There's no one outside. Everyone has long since left."

The pub was brightly lit, warm, and noisy. Seated across from Willie Sloan at a scarred oak table, she ordered a glass of wine.

"From whom are you running, Miss Leighton," Willie asked.

"What makes you think I'm running?" she demanded, her eyes widening in surprise.

"Several reasons. It doesn't take much intuition to sense that there is something very much amiss. At first I wondered why the glamorous Miss Leighton would agree to join a company that is hardly distinguished. Next, I overheard you instructing the doorman to allow no one to be admitted to your dressing room tonight. Then, when I was fortunate enough to gain admittance, I saw a red rose lying on the floor. All of this led me to the conclusion that you are a most unhappy and lonely young lady, who needs a shoulder to cry on, or at the very least someone to talk to for a while. Now drink your wine and let me make an earnest attempt to cheer you up."

Toria laughed. "Thank you, Willie," she said quietly. "You're right, of course. This evening I desperately need a friend, although I promise I won't cry on your shoulder."

"It would be a pleasure!" He sipped his beer and gave her a shy smile.

"Toria, I wish to see you alone." Alex made no attempt to lower his voice as he approached their table, and the conversation in the crowded pub died down to a whisper as all eyes focused on him.

Toria did not glance up from her glass of wine, and

when Willie Sloan stirred uncomfortably in his chair, starting to rise, she said in her clear, high voice, "Stay, Willie. Finish your pint of beer. Whatever the Duke of Blakesley has to say can be said in your presence." Her violet eyes had become as cold and hard as steel. She held her head high. Her cheeks were fiery red and her hands unsteady as she lifted the glass of wine to her lips. "I can't imagine, Alex," she finally said, "why you would wish to see me."

"To apologize."

She gave a mirthless laugh. "I'm weary of your apologies."

Alex cast an uneasy glance at Willie Sloan before plunging onward. "I came to tell you that I love you, Victoria."

"Oh, yes, you did mention that on the card I received tonight. All right, you love me, but as I've heard that before, I'm surprised you made the trip all the way from London to deliver the message. A letter through the post would have certainly sufficed. By the way, how is Lady Caroline? I assume the engagement, which was off, is on again."

Willie Sloan cleared his throat and stood up, balancing himself awkwardly first on one foot, then the other. Neither of them heard him mumble good night. They were too intent on staring at each other —her eyes scornful, his troubled—each separated from the other by a wide abyss of misunderstanding.

"Alex, I can't bear any more of this," she said, her voice so low that he had to lean across the table to hear her.

"Victoria," he replied, "I ask of you three questions. Will you forgive me? Will you love me? Will you marry me?"

Miraculously her anger, her utter misery, her complete despair vanished as a light snow dissolves in early spring.

"Oh, Alex, my darling, yes, yes, yes!" she cried.

In full view of a crowded room in a local pub in Liverpool, the Duke of Blakesley gathered Victoria into his arms. There was amused laughter, and light applause as Alex and Victoria walked out of the pub, hand in hand, into the darkness of the night.

Victoria and Alexander were married the following week in the ancient chapel at Uplands. It was a simple ceremony, with Ann her only attendant, and the Duchess of Blakesley proudly standing nearby in the family pew.

After a journey to Italy, they returned to England, and as the years passed, spent more and more of their time at Uplands, preferring its peaceful surroundings to Mayfair's frenetic pace.

Three children were born to them—two sons, Alexander and Rupert, and a daughter named Victoria, who resembled her mother, with the same haunting violet eyes and glorious golden hair.

Now and then Toria met the Prince of Wales at functions in London or on weekends in the country. She was at Westminster Abbey when he was crowned king, while Alex, splendid in his scarlet robes, took part in the spectacular ceremony.

On several occasions when she met the king, he requested her to sing. As she did, she was intrigued by the expression of sadness, of nostalgia for bygone days reflected in his eyes.

One glorious spring morning when she and Alex rode together through the woods at Uplands, Victoria said to him with a mischievous smile, "Alex, sometimes it worries me that I will never be able to tell our children the name of my father. Obviously, they are far too young now to be curious, but someday soon they are bound to ask me all sorts of uncomfortable questions which I won't be able to answer."

He gave her an amused glance. "You are usually so clever, Victoria. Haven't you guessed?"

"Oh, I've guessed," she replied with a light laugh, "but the trouble is, if my guess is correct, the situation becomes all the more complicated—for then, of course, I could never reveal to them the name of their grandfather."

THE WILD ONE

by
MARIANNE HARVEY
bestselling author of *The Dark Horseman*
and *The Proud Hunter*

Proud, beautiful Judith—raised by her stern
grandmother on the savage Cornish coast—
boldly abandoned herself to one man and sought
solace in the arms of another. But only one man
could tame her, could match her fiery spirit,
could fulfill the passionate promise of rapturous,
timeless love.

A Dell Book $2.95   (19207-2)

THE DARK HORSEMAN

Marianne Harvey
author of *The Proud Hunter*

Beautiful Donna Penroze had sworn to her dying father that she would save her sole legacy, the crumbling tin mines and the ancient, desolate estate *Trencobban*. But the mines were failing, and Donna had no one to turn to. No one except the mysterious Nicholas Trevarvas—rich, arrogant, commanding. Donna would do anything but surrender her pride, anything but admit her irresistible longing for *The Dark Horseman*.

A Dell Book $3.25

Love—the way you want it!

Candlelight Romances

Dell Bestsellers

- [ ] **RANDOM WINDS** by Belva Plain $3.50 (17158-X)
- [ ] **MEN IN LOVE** by Nancy Friday $3.50 (15404-9)
- [ ] **JAILBIRD** by Kurt Vonnegut $3.25 (15447-2)
- [ ] **LOVE: Poems** by Danielle Steel $2.50 (15377-8)
- [ ] **SHOGUN** by James Clavell $3.50 (17800-2)
- [ ] **WILL** by G. Gordon Liddy $3.50 (09666-9)
- [ ] **THE ESTABLISHMENT** by Howard Fast........$3.25 (12296-1)
- [ ] **LIGHT OF LOVE** by Barbara Cartland $2.50 (15402-2)
- [ ] **SERPENTINE** by Thomas Thompson $3.50 (17611-5)
- [ ] **MY MOTHER/MY SELF** by Nancy Friday $3.25 (15663-7)
- [ ] **EVERGREEN** by Belva Plain $3.50 (13278-9)
- [ ] **THE WINDSOR STORY**
  by J. Bryan III & Charles J.V. Murphy $3.75 (19346-X)
- [ ] **THE PROUD HUNTER** by Marianne Harvey ..$3.25 (17098-2)
- [ ] **HIT ME WITH A RAINBOW**
  by James Kirkwood $3.25 (13622-9)
- [ ] **MIDNIGHT MOVIES** by David Kaufelt $2.75 (15728-5)
- [ ] **THE DEBRIEFING** by Robert Litell $2.75 (01873-5)
- [ ] **SHAMAN'S DAUGHTER** by Nan Salerno
  & Rosamond Vanderburgh $3.25 (17863-0)
- [ ] **WOMAN OF TEXAS** by R.T. Stevens $2.95 (19555-1)
- [ ] **DEVIL'S LOVE** by Lane Harris $2.95 (11915-4)

At your local bookstore or use this handy coupon for ordering:

DELL BOOKS
P.O. BOX 1000, PINEBROOK, N.J. 07058

Please send me the books I have checked above. I am enclosing $ _____
(please add 75¢ per copy to cover postage and handling). Send check or money
order—no cash or C.O.D.'s. Please allow up to 8 weeks for shipment.

Mr/Mrs/Miss _____

Address _____

City _____ State/Zip _____